Joel T. Cruz

January 2006

COPY CATS

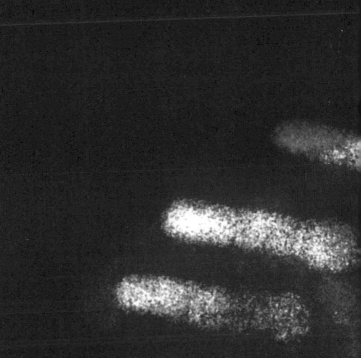

COPY CATS

STORIES
BY
DAVID
CROUSE

THE UNIVERSITY OF GEORGIA PRESS | ATHENS AND LONDON

Published by the University of Georgia Press

Athens, Georgia 30602

© 2005 by David Crouse

All rights reserved

Designed by Mindy Basinger Hill

Set in Electra

Printed and bound by Maple-Vail

Printed in the United States of America

09 08 07 06 05 C 5 4 3 2 1

Library of Congress Cataloging-in-Publication Data

Crouse, David.

Copy cats : stories / by David Crouse.

    p. cm. — (The Flannery O'Connor Award for Short Fiction)

ISBN 0-8203-2746-8 (hardback : alk. paper)

1. Psychological fiction, American. 2. Alienation (Social psychology) —

Fiction. I. Title. II. Series.

PS3603.R685C67 2005

813'.6 — dc22   2005005289

ISBN-13 978-0-8203-2746-4 (hardback ; alk. paper)

British Library Cataloging-in-Publication Data available

For Melina, with much love,
and for Dylan, in the year of your birth

CONTENTS

ACKNOWLEDGMENTS

Some of these stories first appeared in slightly different form in the following publications: *Laurel Review*, "Retreat"; *Massachusetts Review*, "Code"; *Northwest Review*, "Kopy Kats" and "Swimming in the Dark" (titled as "Worlds Apart"); *Quarterly West*, "Click" and "Morte Infinita."

Thanks to the Massachusetts Cultural Council for a grant aiding in the completion of the stories in this collection.

Thanks to my friends and family for their support: my parents Alfred and Marie Crouse, Perry Glasser, Jennifer Barber, Greg Moutafis, Jon Dembling, Kerstin Mueller, Brad and Kelly Mintz, Rusty Dolleman, Adam Spector, Dylan Hall, Peggy Walsh, Roger Benson, Craig Harriman, Tigh Rickman, Jessica Bryant, Robert Jones, and my students, both past and present.

"do you want to hear about what happened to me today or not?"

"Sure," she said. He wasn't sure if she was listening. She was looking at the television and rolling her second or third joint and probably getting ready to say something about Mom, who was a professor of applied sciences, and Dad, who was a professor of human studies. An open shoebox sat atop the TV. They had sent her something again.

He walked over to the fish tank and tapped on the glass at the tarantula sitting motionless on its sand-speckled brick. It looked as plastic as his toys. "How long do these things live?" Anthony had asked Johnny Valhouli when he had shown up with it in the pocket of his raincoat, and Johnny had wiped the back of his arm across his nose and answered, "A couple hundred years. Three hundred years sometimes."

It had been an interesting lie, and Anthony passed it along to Vanessa, who passed it along to her gonzo fanzine-reading buddies in Allston. He liked to think the story had spread all over the place, like the one about the time he pissed in the reservoir. He crouched down on the rug, as if he were about to pounce, but did not know what to say except to repeat himself. "Let me tell you about what happened," he said. "I can talk and you can listen."

"Oh, yeah?" she said.

"Yeah," he said.

"Okay, tell me about it," she said, and so he did. He told her about Yorick falling and the paramedics pushing through the door. He told her about the circus atmosphere and the flatness of the next couple of hours at work and then the long trip on the subway, because the story didn't end when the ambulance

She liked to change his words around a little and speak them back to him so that she could watch him smile and nod at their wisdom.

"I can't go in," he said, looking into the rearview mirror at the theater marquee. He smiled tightly without taking his hands off the wheel, as if they were still driving down the road. "I can't go in there with those people. I just can't." He was crying. He leaned back his head, let out a deep breath, and said, "Oh boy."

She pictured the inside of his head as a labyrinth where he would sometimes get lost. The houses he designed were smooth and made with lots of glass, beautiful and transparent and cold and not at all the kind of place most people would want to live. She wondered if his brain was too full of these beautiful buildings, variations of shape and form and function and strange angles like a whole other neighborhood that existed and did not exist. That was where he spent most of his time lately.

Her mother—she resided in sunnier climes.

When little Edward Eisenstein introduced Kristen to *Morte Infinita* that Halloween—the Halloween her father lifted the rock and smiled as if he were the daddy of all vampires—well, it was a revelation, what her father would have called the opening of the mind to new frontiers. On the 29th of October her mother had called from Florida, and for two days Kristen had searched for meaning in each one of her father's pinched expressions. But then on Halloween afternoon in the Eisensteins' furnished basement the haze lifted, and it was like, oh yeah, man. It was like before and after pictures in the back of comic books.

"This is the kind of movie even *your* dad wouldn't let you

I don't know—indistinctness of vision. But that doesn't mean you shouldn't be careful. That's not what I'm saying. Remember what Kierkegaard said. 'The torment of despair is not to be able to die. To be sick unto death is not to be able to die.'"

That was the way he spoke to her, as if she were forty years old and four years old, making references to philosophers with names like curses and explaining that ice cream was really bad for her. It was like he couldn't get a bead on the place in the universe she was right now. He shot too long or too short—at various future and past selves—and he could never find his true target: a thirteen-year-old girl with braces who just a few days before had slapped a freckle-faced boy on the side of the head and then spit at the school principal when he tried to break it up. What had her mother asked her the night before she left? "Kristen, are you angry?"

Kristen had a new idea, and she tried the thought on for size the way she sometimes tried on ugly clothing at the mall—just to see how bad it looked. Her mother had died from a horrible illness. It was one of those devastating dark age kind of diseases, a dawn-of-time pestilence sort of thing. Her father sat across from her, simmering in his grief, which was natural, even kind of noble, and Kristen had to be strong, because his love had made him weak.

But halfway through the second waffle she felt the first waffle hardening in her tummy, and she pictured her mother embraced by brawny sailor's arms—the arms of the hero—as if this were the end of a Hollywood movie and the credits were about to roll. But it was not the end. It was the beginning, right?

"The name of the movie is *Morte Infinita*," Eisenstein said two days later on Halloween afternoon as they moved around the side of his house to the cellar. They let themselves in—the back-door was unlocked—and he popped the tape in and clicked on the TV. Kristen pushed a square of cardboard against the nearest window to block the sunshine. Children and parents would be roaming the darkened streets in a couple of hours, and then they would return to their houses and take off their costumes and be in bed by ten o'clock. The next morning it would be sunshine and morning newspapers and kisses on the cheek, but right then the ground was beginning to break open like something ripe. Zombies. Foreign zombies. The TV was full of them. "Is that Spanish?" Kristen asked.

"It's Italian," Eisenstein said, and then he pronounced the words with relish, *Morte Infinita,* as if he were pronouncing the name of a complicated Italian dish. She reached into the bag on the cushion between them. The cheese snacks left orange dust on her fingers. She sucked them clean, one at a time, as she leaned forward. The zombies scrambled over shattered bricks and along the banks of dried-up rivers. Without people to kill they were sad and lost and innocent as babies. She was reminded of her mother's voice on the phone a couple of days before. At the time it had seemed normal. But after the fact, in her memory, it sounded desperately hopeful, like the voice of a person on a game show trying to figure out the right answer. "I needed to get away for a little while," she had said. "I hope you understand. Your father will take care of you. He will. Is he taking good care of you? He's not good at much, I guess, but he's good at taking care of you. Sometimes, I think, better than me. But I'm sure you don't think that. Is he there?"

When the prettiest woman in the cast was killed twenty minutes in, Kristen knew she was in for something special. When the sliver of wood penetrated the eye of the local doctor and the camera zoomed in and held the shot and the music swelled as if something romantic had just happened, Kristen felt her heart beating strong and fast. When a zombie in a tattered priest's robe took a chunk from the hero's neck and he was lost in a sea of rotting corpses, well, God bless Anthony Fentana, the director of the movie and writer of the screenplay, a man who was probably dead himself in an Italian cemetery. The disjointed plot, the graininess of the film, the detail of the gore, all of it confirmed something. "That was *amazing*," she said as the screen turned black and then sky blue.

Eisenstein said, "What did I tell you? There's nothing like the Europeans when it comes to zombie movies." He took off his black-framed glasses—he wore them only when watching television—and Kristen could see from his tentative toad-lipped expression that she had been called here for other purposes. The week before, he had tried to put his arm around her while they were watching *The Angry Red Planet*, and she had bent forward and laughed. It wasn't like he was a jerk or anything, or that repulsive even, although he had a weak chin and greasy, feathered hair. But there was something about him that would probably make girls laugh until he was middle-aged, and Kristen guessed he knew this too. "Kristen?" he said.

"Yes?"

"Do you love me?"

"Of course not," she said. It was enough to make her smack him. Jesus Christ.

"I know," he said, and they listened to the video rewind.

"Kristen?" he said after a while.

"What?"

"I'm sorry," he said.

"Don't worry about it." She reached out and touched him on the shoulder and thought about how young he seemed in his spindly puberty. She saw him as a different species altogether, something slow moving and amphibious and sensitive to light. His father was a big man with a truck driver's body, but he worked as a consultant for insurance companies, making spreadsheets and graphs and giving presentations about the statistical likelihood of people dying from this or that or the other thing. Little Eisenstein would probably end up doing something similar.

"I wish there was something I could do to help," Eisenstein said.

"Help with what?"

"Everything," he said, and the crack in his voice made her want to wrap her arms around him and squeeze. He said, "My dad was talking about having you stay at our place until your mother comes back."

The window shades were down day and night, but their lives were still on display as if they lived in one of her dad's glass buildings. She said, "Your father also said that the Red Sox were going to win a pennant last year. I remember him telling us that. Do you remember that?"

"Yeah," he said.

She said, "Did your dad mention anything about Stephanos? Is he coming back with her?"

"Who?" he asked, and she told him never mind, and then she made her hands into fists and played drums on her knees, and they were quiet except for the music she made on her body.

"I'm just trying to help," he said finally.

"If you want to help then just sit quietly." She sounded like his mother or teacher or some stupid thing. The idea of her needing Eisenstein's help made her feel small, like he could lift her up in his hands. Her father was not a big man, but he was bigger on the inside than the outside, as if he followed some extradimensional logic. She was the same way. They could handle this together. They always had, right down the line.

"But Kristen," Eisenstein said. His voice was whiny with love and goodwill. She cut him off with a shush, and then they were quiet. It was a perfect moment.

Then she said, "Let's watch the movie again." He found the remote and the opening music began to play, plodding piano chords like something shambling and aimless. She watched Eisenstein's face, poor lonely Eisenstein with the 125 IQ and nervous stutter. She turned back to the TV and said, "The blood looks real."

The night her father threw a cloak around his shoulders and told her that they were going trick-or-treating, Kristen had raced against time to be with him. She had taken the short cut from Eisenstein's house. Her bike crashed through the woods, and as she peddled faster she gave out a yelping howl of delight and rage that she hoped people might confuse for something other than a girl of thirteen. It had been a week since her mother left for the airport, and yes, maybe her dad wasn't doing so great, maybe he was in pain, but who gave a shit if he mowed the lawn? And it was wolf pain anyway, the kind of wound that made you smarter and sharper and keener and hungrier and just plain better when everything was done and you were on the other side of it. Leaves and branches snapped against Kristen's face as she sped downhill, and she imagined herself as something dark and mysterious, a one-of-a-kind animal that occupied a solitary ecological niche and was only now deciding to enter the foolish world of mankind.

Her father was in the hall sitting at the desk, writing with the long black feather pen he kept there. "I'm trying to cultivate as many affectations as possible," he sometimes said when using it. She remembered her mother laughing at that joke, the way she threw her head back. Her head was back now too, in bed, Stephanos grunting between her spread legs, his mouth against her shoulder like it was an apple. Kristen had seen her father and mother locked in that pose a couple of years ago through the crack in the door.

"Hey," he said, straightening up and looking through her as if she were invisible. "Who goes there? Is that my faithful servant?" That joke again. She knew what was required.

"No," she said.

"It's not my faithful servant?" Mock panic rose in his voice. "Oh, dear. Who then can it be?" He was an effeminate character in a story by Edgar Allan Poe, and she was some deceased relative returning for revenge, dripping water from the pond where she had drowned. She smiled in the dark, and her love became a kind of light by which she could see him clearly.

"No, it's me," she half yelled, and she was suddenly outrageously happy. She wanted to tell him about the movie and the sick, wonderful mind behind it and the blood that looked real and the burning church and the endless body count. She wanted to relive it through his senses. He could show it to her in new ways, open it for her like a book.

He said, "And who are you?"

She said, "You know who I am." She looked at the desk and said, "What are you doing?"

"Writing out a check to the credit card company. It's amazing how expensive your mother's tastes are." With a flourish of his pen he was finished. He cleared his throat and said, "Well, you ready?" She did not know what he meant until he stood up, and she realized he was dressed in the black cloak. "Trick-or-treat," he said. Then they walked downstairs together.

Ghouls and freaks and superheroes smiled at them as they emerged from the house and made their way through the neighborhood. Two Batmans walked side by side toward them. "Neither of them wanted to compromise," their mother explained, and Kristen's father nodded as if he understood. The kids frowned back at Kristen, clutching tightly at their bags of candy. This was serious business. They knew that. Monsters moved in solemn processions of three or four. There was something mournful in the way they walked, as if they were all lost and searching for their homes.

"Here, take these," her father said. He handed her something. Plastic fangs. She was dressed in a black T-shirt and shit kickers. She put the teeth in her mouth, and abracadabra, she was a vampire. "Your mother never enjoyed this kind of thing," Kristen's father said as they walked across the street holding hands. "She was always so afraid that someone was going to get hit by a car."

He was talking as if her mother was dead. For a ridiculous split second Kristen wondered if he had read her mind in the diner when she had considered the same thing. "Dad?" she asked.

"Yes?"

"How did Mom meet what's-his-face?"

His lips pursed slightly. He was thinking.

"Dad?" she asked.

"Yes?" he said.

"You're in a lot of trouble, aren't you?"

"That's a hard question to answer," he said. "I'm not sure."

g, her eyes shut tight. She thought of their conversation a few
ays before, her father's pleading voice. How many things like
his had Kristen missed—moments when the door was closed or
he words were exchanged late at night when she was sleeping?
or each she had seen there must have been a hundred that
ad slipped past her. "What about Stephanos?" she asked, and
here was a sharp edge to her words. Her own voice startled her.

Her father scowled as if he had forgotten this important part
f the equation, and then he said, "Don't worry about him.
He's just a fling. That's all he is." Then he straightened up,
moothed out his cloak, and headed up the steps to the front
loor of their destination. He knocked three times and stepped
back, raising both arms in the air ready to strike.

Mrs. Van Dyke seemed surprised to see them, but she opened
the screen door and smiled. "We're supposed to be vampires,"
Kristen said quietly, and she opened her mouth to show off the
teeth. She was too old for this.

"Oh, yes," Mrs. Van Dyke said, and she handed her an apple
and a Snickers bar. They thanked her and walked away, back
down the steps, Kristen feeling the woman's farsighted eyes on
her back.

A few houses were dark, and Kristen wondered what was
inside them, behind the window shades, down their cellars.
Most, though, were lit up with orange light, or decorated with
paper witches and ghosts. A few played eerie music from open
doors or recordings of people screaming and evil laughter. Two
big beefy kids passed by wearing hockey masks as costumes,
and although Kristen vaguely recognized them, their real faces
were hard to remember. The same with the skinny Darth Vader
who ran up Mrs. Van Dyke's stairs as they were heading down.
Was he from her homeroom?

He squeezed her hand a little more tightly. T
a brightly colored spaceman holding a plastic
dad made a sound like he was eating candy
noise, but he didn't say anything else until th
sidewalk on the other side of the street. Then
bent down and looked in her eyes the way a
might before a batter goes to the plate. He sa
steady and reasonable-sounding voice she had h
all week, "Your mother and I met sixteen years a;
three, and she was twenty-two. That's a big difl
almost your whole life, kiddo. You don't just th
because someone's hit a rough patch." He put
mouth, as if he was about to clear his throat.
there was no other guy involved in this mess. Ju:
and your mother. That still wouldn't be an excu
in this day and age. There are medications. Ther
crap. Analysis and stuff. Aromatherapy, for Chri
began to laugh, and he rubbed the top of her h
knuckles. "We live in an enlightened age, after al

She did not want this. She wanted an answer
keep looking into his eyes until he gave her on
"Dad, are you getting better?"

He looked at her as if she had just said somethin
and amusing. He said, "You wouldn't remember,
this a couple of times when you were this big." I
thumb and finger apart an inch, as if he was holdi
a screw or some small thing that could be lost if y
"I wouldn't be surprised if things were back to nori
week," he said.

She remembered again her mother's craned ne
the crack in the door, head tilted back as if posing i

"Don't eat the apple," her dad said as they walked away from the house. "I don't trust that Mrs. Van Dyke. She could snap any minute." He took the apple and bit into it with a little growl. "How is school going these days?" he asked between chews. "That hillbilly kid, is he still picking on you?"

"A little," she said.

"He only does that because he likes you."

"No, he hates me," Kristen said. "He wants to stomp me into mulch. I can see it in his eyes." She didn't mention that he had also insulted her dad, calling him a mental patient. That's what had made her rain punches on his gross freckled face and then spit at the principal when he had interfered with what was really a question of honor.

"That's just his way of showing you that he has a crush on you," her dad explained.

She stopped and spit her teeth into her hand so she could speak more easily. "The costumes suck this year," she said. "Maybe it's just that I'm getting older."

Nobody came to the door of the next house, although the porch light was on and she had seen other eager people receiving candy there. Her dad tapped on the window with his knuckles, threw his coat around his shoulder in a gesture of exaggerated indignation, and walked down the steps. She followed him to the Eisensteins' house, where she knew sad little Eisenstein was watching *Morte Infinita* for the third time. She popped the teeth back in her mouth and nudged them into position with her tongue.

"We're vampires, Charlie," Kristen's father said to Eisenstein's dad when he opened the door. "Don't invite us in, for God's sake. Put garlic in your windows and get a cross. We've come for you and your wife and son, but especially for your wife."

"Very funny," Mr. Eisenstein said. "Do you want to come in, or do you just want some candy?" He was holding a bag of mini 3 Musketeers in his hand. Kristen could hear the television playing in the living room, some voice talking about a helicopter disaster. She didn't know where or who or how, just that it had happened. She looked at her father, who was smiling tightly, the way he had that day outside the movie festival.

Mr. Eisenstein said, "Do you want a beer?" and moved back from the door.

"No, thanks," her dad said, "but I bet Kristen wants some of those delicious 3 Musketeers." They stepped into the house.

"I bet I don't," she said. She was looking around for Eisenstein himself peeking around a corner or something, but he was probably in the cellar. She saw evidence of him, though, in the little black sneakers in the entranceway. She hadn't realized his feet were so small.

"I'm surprised to see you here," Eisenstein's dad said to her father.

Kristen's dad smiled and looked around the room, at the photographs of their dog and brothers and grandparents and great-aunts—their entire history on display. "Yeah, well, that's the way it is with vampires. We rely heavily on the element of surprise."

Eisenstein's dad made a sound like he had something stuck in his throat, and for a second Kristen thought candy was lodged down there somewhere, but then he said, "Are you treating her well?" He didn't look in her direction, but Kristen knew he was talking about her, and she had the momentary feeling that her body was back home and only her spirit was here as an observer. She wondered what part of the movie Eisenstein was watching and what he meant when he said he loved her. Her mother had used that word many times and so had her father. Kristen loved her father and loved *Morte Infinita*, and she wanted to be alone with one or the other, not standing here listening to Mr. Eisenstein. "She looks skinny," he said. "She looks like she's getting thinner."

"Vampires are thin," her dad said and then, "Have you talked to my wife lately, Charlie? Does she deign to call you from paradise?"

"Paradise?" Mr. Eisenstein said.

"Just a little joke."

"I don't get it."

"Does she call you?"

"She called me once, a few days ago. She was concerned about you. She said you sounded funny." There was something apologetic in his voice. "I'm sorry. You're putting me in a difficult position here."

"My wife knows a lot about difficult positions," her dad said. "And she's still my wife, you know. And Kristen is still my daughter." Then he laughed as if something funny had been said on the television, but the announcers were still going on about the helicopter accident. She wondered if someone famous had been killed.

"Come on," Mr. Eisenstein said. "Let's not start."

Kristen's father was looking at a magazine on the coffee table. The cover of the magazine showed a smiling young woman dressed in a bright sweatshirt and little yellow shorts. She was touching her toes and smiling. From the expression on his face, Kristen's dad looked as if he had suddenly recognized this woman and was now remembering something awful she had done to him once. He went to the table and picked up the magazine. Leafing through it he said, "Don't pretend you know what's good for her. That's all I'm saying."

Closing the door Mr. Eisenstein came and looked at the magazine as if he wanted to read it next.

"I thought you were doing okay," he said. "I wanted to give you the benefit of the doubt. I really did."

"I wanted to give you the benefit of the doubt too," her dad said, his voice high and mocking, "but I'm pretty curious why you're protecting her. I've seen the way you two flirt. Don't pretend you don't."

Eisenstein's dad laughed then, arms folded across his chest. He looked down at the floor, at his shoelaces, at the zigzag pattern in the carpet. "This is ridiculous," he said.

"Are you fucking her?" Kristin's dad said. "Or do you just *want* to fuck her?"

Kristen thought of her mother walking hand in hand with her new boyfriend on some stoneless beach and wanted to believe it because it was what her father had told her. She looked at him turning the pages of the magazine, his body draped in black, and loved him so fiercely that she wanted to tear at his clothes and dig down into those hidden places and find the darkness there and grab it like a tumor. Mr. Eisenstein said, "You're going through some tough times. I understand that. But turning it into a performance piece is only going to make it worse."

"I don't think you understand," her dad said. "I didn't make it into theater. You made it into theater. Cheryl made it into theater. You're the ones who put me on stage. Do you think I wanted that?"

Kristen knew she had left his mind, his imagination. She was invisible, but there was no power in that.

"She was worried," Mr. Eisenstein said, "so she made a god-damned phone call."

Her dad dropped the magazine to the table and looked at Mr. Eisenstein in the same way he had been looking at the girl on the cover. "She's worried about herself. That's who she's worried about."

"About you too. And Kristen."

"Which is why she left."

"You were wearing her down. You know that. She needed a break. Jesus, you're wearing me down, and we've only been talking for five minutes."

"It's my problem," he said. "Not yours. Not hers."

"That's just stupid," Mr. Eisenstein said. "You think you could keep it private? It's like you're living in a fantasy world."

"Well, I'm sorry about that," her dad said, "but I like it here," and he laughed again. Kristen moved over to the window and looked out at the street, where a few more mermaids and Tinkerbells and cardboard robots were coming up the sidewalk. Why did they all look mad?

Mr. Eisenstein said, "You may be unwell, and that's fine, but you're also a prick. Get out of my house."

Her father smiled and took a step toward Mr. Eisenstein, and Mr. Eisenstein flinched the way his son sometimes did in the schoolyard. Even though he was bigger than her dad, even though it was his house they were standing in, he was the one who was afraid.

Kristen wanted to tell him to cut it out, that it was just her dad, her dad who dreamed about buildings and never hurt anybody.

The doorbell was ringing. One time. Twice. Three and then four times. Her father laughed and pulled his cloak in front of himself in the manner of Bela Lugosi and took another step forward, but his movements were exaggerated. They were funny. It was Dracula as played by Groucho Marx. It was definitely not *Morte Infinita* or even *Nosferatu*. "You see, you see, you see," Kristen wanted to say. There was no danger in him.

The two men looked at each other and then turned away.

"Mom doesn't *have* a boyfriend, does she?" she asked as they were walking down the steps back to the street.

He turned his back to her, hunching his shoulders, and she thought of the first horror film she had ever seen, years before on late-night cable. At the end of the movie the villain had spun away from the crowd and staggered off into the shadows, trying to hide his acid-scarred face from the stares of his loved ones. But her father didn't move.

She listened to him make muffled baby sounds, and after a few moments she took him by the hand, and they walked across the lawn. Mr. Eisenstein was watching them from the window. Then the curtains closed, and the porch light blinked off, and she thought of Eisenstein down in the basement and then of Stephanos, the imaginary man who had been so vivid to her. Her father had hexed him into existence with some sleight of hand—a bunch of words was all it took.

And if he did not exist, then in a strange way her father did not exist—at least not the person she thought she had known. She looked at him, one hand rubbing his reddened eyes, the other gripping her hand, and was surprised that she loved him even more. She gripped him back, but he stepped away from her and picked up the rock. "There are two kinds of people in this world," he said, and he grinned his Dracula grin. And he was right. She wanted him to be right.

Two kinds of people in the world. You were either a vampire or a zombie, and just like in the movies, the zombies were many, many, and the vampires were few and far between. And although the zombies had the numbers, the vampires had class and skill. They lived on the margins, peeking in from time to time when it suited them or pretending they were not vampires at all. She wanted so much to believe.

Kristen was a vampire—she knew that now more surely than ever before—and as she ran down the street, the faces of ghouls and Raggedy Anns and blue-skinned Smurfs and superheroes all turned in her direction. Faces of parents too, holding hands with transformed daughters and sons and suddenly shocked alert by the breaking of glass and the yapping of the Eisensteins' Labrador retriever. They were all zombies really, and she despised each and every one of them almost as much as she hated her mother and her imaginary boyfriend. She hated them for not being what her father called on them to be. She hated them the way she hated the victims in horror movies, and herself, for running so quickly without thinking about whom she had left behind.

Remembering the movie. That's what brought her around the house to the bulkhead, where she rattled the double doors. She could hear yelling from the front of the house. Eisenstein said, "Who is it?"

"It's me," she said, but the doors did not open. She tried to picture herself as a vampire and Eisenstein as the innocent victim struggling to resist her. She wanted to hold him and bury her face in his pale neck and swallow and swallow until she felt better—until his innocent blood mixed with her own. "Open up," she said in her most confident singsong voice, but it came out wrong. It sounded afraid and frail and as human as human can be, and for a second she did not recognize it.

People were running up the street toward the window her father had just shattered, and Kristen tried to think of her mother on her sailboat, but all she could see in her mind's eye was the rock on the Eisensteins' shag rug. She banged on the door until her hand hurt. She tried to make her clatter a match for the noise on the other side of the house, where her father must have been doing something else to make people yell. She spit her teeth into the grass. She gave the door a kick. "It's me!" she hollered.

"Who?" Eisenstein said.

"It's Kristen," she said. "Just Kristen," and the door opened and she stepped inside.

A close-up of Stephanie's face. The pockmarks in her cheeks, a slender scar on her temple, lips puckered like a model's, but something dangerous in the eyes. Stephanie standing in front of a white drop cloth. Stephanie naked with her arms above her head so that she looks flat chested and boyish. Stephanie blowing smoke into the camera.

She said, "None of these pictures look like me."

He said, "How about this one?"

He showed her another close-up, one where she was looking to the right and grinning so that crow's-feet formed at the corners of her eyes. She looked older in that picture but pretty, the lines in her face more natural somehow, as if they were caused by motherhood and sunshine.

They sat staring down at her kitchen table like they were searching for something. More than a dozen photographs lay scattered there. They had cleared space by pushing aside the morning's cereal bowl and a weekend's worth of dirty glasses smelling of rum and Coca-Cola.

She moved the photos around and then picked up another, seemingly at random. In this one her arms were behind her back, her head slightly raised. The drop cloth spread behind her replaced the background clutter with a simple white sheen.

She said, "I have a funny expression on my face. I look scared."

The cloth was an idea he swiped from Richard Avedon's fashion photography, and it had worked pretty well. These shots were some of his favorites because they balanced the others—the needles, the pipes, the brightly colored depression medication, her shirtless body with its complex challenge. Look away or look, either way you're wrong.

She put down the photo and said, "Are you hungry?"

He smiled. "What do you have?" It was good—and humbling—to accept food from someone who didn't have much.

Three things in her freezer—a container of orange sherbet, a one-pound can of cheap coffee, and a package of film he had left there as backup. The combination seemed to say something profound about her, although what it was exactly he didn't know.

She said, "Rashid and his brother are eating me out of house and home."

When she was feeling desperate or frivolous, she gave hand jobs to men in parked cars in exchange for food. The cars were in the lot behind her house right now. The men had just started the second shift in the metal shop across the street. He had photographs of some of them. He had photographs of her afterward, holding McDonald's bags and drinking strawberry milk shakes.

She was laughing now. She said, "I don't believe it. I sound like my mother."

He thought, there's something almost clandestine about leaving film here, something *intimate*. He sat down again and looked at the photographs and suddenly they seemed not very good at all. He had several hundred of them spread out on the table in the basement at home, hung by clothespins along a wire, organized in files, and stuffed into the drawers of an old bureau. But none of them seemed to be exactly what he was looking for. Something was eluding him.

"Jesus," she said. She was slapping the photos on the table one at time now as if she were dealing out cards.

He noticed the jug of milk and half-eaten Cheerios by the sink, and he had to fight the urge to record it for posterity—the primitive flowers painted around the edge of the bowl, the white soured crust ringing the mouth of the jug.

"Is this how you see me?" she asked, nodding her head slowly, almost sagely, like someone trying to appear old and wise, although she was only in her midthirties, not much older than he was. Then she produced a joint from somewhere and lit it up. She closed her eyes and took a long hit. This was the message for him to leave.

On the way down the back steps he turned sideways for two teenagers making their way up. They wore identical Raiders caps and camouflage jackets, and as they passed him one said something to make the other laugh. He wondered if he was the punch line to the joke. When he had first started taking shots inside Stephanie's apartment a month or so ago, these same kids—or kids who looked a lot like them—had hung around his car smoking cigarettes. Now he parked a couple of blocks away and walked to her place, camera in the inside pocket of his leather jacket. It was okay to play it safe. It said nothing about him except that he was cautious.

A small road ran between the backside of the old factories and the Merrimack River, and as he slipped the car into drive and looked over his shoulder, he decided to head home by that route. A pair of sneakers had been tied together by their shoelaces and thrown over a telephone wire nearly a year ago, and he was oddly inspired to see them still dangling there, twirling in the wind. His car moved under them and then under the pigeon-swarmed undercarriage of a small steel bridge, and he turned and followed the concrete wall built between the water and the road. Past the wet mattresses and empty husks of televisions the road grew narrower, and he slowed and watched the river to his right. It was moving quickly today, and he thought of Stephanie's half-closed eyes, the way she had smiled up at him from her chair at the table. She had said, "Could you take the trash down with you when you go?" She had said, "Thanks. Thanks for everything."

She was always like that when she first saw the pictures, like a drunk suddenly remembering what she had done the night before. She had willingly agreed to all the poses, had even suggested some of them herself, with that one-sided smile she sometimes flashed at unexpected moments. *So you want to see something? I'll show you something.*

The first time Jonathan saw her had been in early April, when piles of dirty snow were still melting at the edges of the grocery store parking lots. He noticed her near the Goodwill bins, stuffing clothing into a black trash bag. He stood by his car, his keys in one hand, paper bag of groceries in the other, and he watched her.

Her hair was hidden and so was her body. She wore a heavy black hooded coat, unbuttoned, and a baseball cap. At first he thought it was an elderly man, but when she dropped the bag and bent down to gather it up, he decided it was a little boy, some lean, hard-eyed runaway.

"Hurry back," Margaret had said from the couch as he went out the door.

Jonathan always seemed to be running behind, and this time was no exception, but he didn't care. Let Margaret's friends wait for him, and for the whipped cream and strawberries he said he was going to bring back, and for the little story of what he was watching over at the dumpster, because he would bring that back for them too.

He set the groceries on the hood of his car, and she reached her hand up inside the bin and fished around, standing on her toes. He thought she might be crazy. A crazy old man or a kid. No, a woman. He saw that now. Her cap had blown off her head. She bent down, picked it up, and shoved it into her pocket. Nobody else was watching, although the parking lot was full of cars. Something about her was invisible, as if she were a figment of his imagination.

The bin was filled to overflowing, and she could reach and grab and pull things free—children's sneakers tied together by the laces, an old sweatshirt, a broken umbrella she struggled with and then tossed onto the pavement in disgust. When she raised both hands above her head, she seemed to be trying to climb up into the bin. The illusion was so convincing that for a second he thought she might live there, which was ridiculous

sink, and he wanted to get to it before Margaret poured it down the drain.

"Can you get me one too?" the wife said. "A vodka and tonic?"

"Sure," he said, not intending to, and pushed the thought out of his mind as he turned around and beat his way back to the kitchen. A few more people had arrived and were taking off their coats. He had never seen them before.

Mrs. Accountant looked at him seriously when he returned. "What?" he asked.

"The drink?"

"Oh, yeah," he said and gave her his beer. The accountant and someone else were talking about the stock market, and she was probably feeling left out. She took the beer, and Jonathan smiled at her and touched two fingers to his temple in salute. "A toast," he said. "To the beautiful people in Hollywood. We love them. And they love us."

"It's wounded, but it's not dead," he heard the accountant say.

"I hate all our friends," he told Margaret that night in bed.

She kissed him on the chest, then sat up and made her way across him until she was straddling his stomach. Her hair was tied back, and her cheeks and forehead were shiny with moisturizer. She was, he decided, incredibly beautiful. "You hate all *my* friends is what you mean."

"Yeah," he said with a laugh. "Where do you find these people?"

"Out there," she said with a little gesture at the shaded window. "There are all sorts of people in the world. Billions of them, I've heard. Sometimes it's interesting to have conversations with them. They ask you if you've seen any good movies lately. You make a joke, and then they make a joke. They say,

'Remember that time?' and you say, 'Oh, yeah.' That kind of thing. You should try it sometime."

"Maybe," he said, serious all of a sudden.

"Maybe," she said, imitating his somber voice.

In early January, when dried Christmas trees began to appear in the garbage in front of the three-story apartment buildings along Water Street, Jonathan called her up and said, "Stephanie, I have a new idea." The weather had grown unseasonably warm, and it had been two weeks since he had been laid off. He had the day free, and he guessed Stephanie did too.

"Sure," she said. "Let's go to the beach."

So Jonathan took pictures of her walking along the boardwalk at Salisbury Beach. She wore a long coat, open down the front, and a dress he had not seen before. She walked with her hands in her pockets, looking in the windows of closed tattoo parlors and pizza joints and video arcades. A stray dog followed them, its fur soaked with salt water, and Stephanie tried out different names on it. Sugar Pea. Devil Scum. Walter Matthau. Little Biscuit. Magnet. The last one stuck, and then the dog stuck to them.

"Magnet," she said, "where's your owner? Did he just up and leave you behind?" She turned it into a song. Her voice was pretty but with an edge, like the photographs he was hoping to take. The wind bit hard despite the sunshine. Her hair was in her eyes and she was hungover, but she was smiling and everything seemed okay.

She told him, "You know, I'm going to be moving soon. I'm going down south to be with my sister."

She was always talking about her sister in Orlando, but she had never mentioned moving before.

"Really?" he said.

They crossed the street lazily at a diagonal. The dog followed them. Jonathan wondered what it was doing for food and how long it had been on its own. There were no cars or other people, and the only thing moving besides themselves and the sea was an orange naval flag whipping in the wind.

"Yes," she said. "Two weeks. Maybe a week. As soon as I can get myself organized." She said the word *organized* slowly, as if she had made it up or were doing a bad imitation of someone—of him maybe.

The dog danced around their feet, lingered behind, caught up with them again. Jonathan's hands were cold. He had used only half a roll of film. Mostly they were just talking.

He smiled. "That's great."

"It *is* great," she said, and she laughed. "Sun and fun. Cute guys. Beaches. Disneyland. Or is it Disney World? Which one is in Orlando?" She kicked at a rock on the sidewalk as if to say, *whatever, it doesn't matter.*

He had been to Orlando once, on one of the tedious business trips his old job had required of him. Although he had spent time only at the convention center and the hotel and the roads in between, he remembered the long stretches of highway with bright strip malls and palm trees on either side. The entire city had seemed like a fantasy, not just Disney World. It was World, right? He was pretty sure it was World.

The dog was sniffing at a spray-painted dumpster. It was hard to tell how healthy it was underneath all that fur.

"Take a picture of me and Magnet," she said.

But the dog wouldn't cooperate. It ran behind the dumpster and made scratching sounds. She called it by its new name. She tried other names. She threw up her hands and laughed.

Two weeks. Maybe less. Well, he had wanted a deadline,

and now he had one. Careful what you wish for, right? Like he needed more pressure.

Stephanie said, "It's because we don't know its real name."

He thought of a photograph he had taken last month, another close-up with her eyes slightly downcast. She had seemed to be letting him in a little in that one, but she had closed up again. She was always opening and closing in some complicated response to the opening and closing of the aperture of his lens.

"Stupid dog," she said, but she was still laughing. She crouched down, her hands on her knees, looking behind some trash cans wrapped in a chain and padlocked. "Ignatius," she said. "Socrates. Fido. Henry."

Maybe she would guess the right one, and something magical would happen. He came up behind her and tried to look where she was looking. "This is going to be good for you. The move."

"Yeah," she said.

There were always errands to run. After he dropped Stephanie off that day, he picked up groceries, which were too expensive of course, and the wedding invitations, which were printed on the wrong paper, white instead of the cream Margaret had ordered, and then headed home by the long route following the river, where every other building was burned out, the windows boarded, the bricks spray-painted with obscenities and coded nicknames. He wasted ten minutes, slowing for yellow lights, driving in circles. When he arrived home, he set down his parcels and immediately went down to the far end of the cellar—to the darkroom he and Margaret had built last summer—where he put on some music, finished the black coffee he had left that morning, and developed the roll.

Stephanie had been standing with her back to the ocean, one hand raised as if to block her face, but the attempt had come too late—her eyes were looking to one side, at the dog out of the frame. That one came the closest of them all—at least today it did. He might change his mind tomorrow. Now as he looked into Stephanie's partially obscured face he could see why people said the eyes were windows to the soul. There was a brightness there that was startling. Some of it was from the catch-light effect caused by the strong flash he had used that day. The rest was ephemeral.

When he looked closer, he found his own blurred face and shoulder reflected in her iris. He was present in all of those shots, like a ghost, like those close-ups by Helmut Newton in which his hands and chest are faintly visible in the eyes of all the movie stars. It was like some subtle joke shared among people who looked closely enough at things.

The fact that she was leaving—that she *might* be leaving—worried him for all sorts of reasons. From the sound of it Stephanie's sister wasn't much better off than she was. And then there were the questions of how Stephanie was going to get there and what she would do when she did get there. Her sister worked the third shift at a 7-Eleven, but he knew Stephanie would never do anything like that. A chump job, she would call it, a job for robots and gimps. No, she'd probably end up scraping together money by selling drugs and her body. But in a sunnier climate. Was that all she wanted—a change of scenery, not a change of life?

Then there was his project. He had a lot of photographs—too many photographs, he sometimes thought—but he wasn't close to being finished, and it was getting harder and harder to put off Margaret. "This is a great opportunity," he had told her when he lost his job. "Think of the unemployment checks as a grant from the state." She had agreed reluctantly with the slight frown that told him she was thinking about something deeply. She knew about Stephanie of course. She had seen the photos, including some of the nudes. One night when they had been drinking at the Mediterranean bar and restaurant, she had looked into her third salt-free margarita and told him to be careful, that Stephanie was out of control, and he had laughed and said, "So are we, Margaret. So are we," not knowing exactly what he meant but liking the idea.

After placing the invitations on the counter in the darkroom, he closed the door and headed upstairs, where he put away the groceries—bottles of bright red curry sauce and overpriced chocolate-dipped biscotti and free-range chicken and egg noodles and oranges almost the size of softballs and half-gallons of low-fat rice milk because Margaret was lactose intolerant. He put an orange to his face and breathed the sharp smell. He wondered if it was from Florida.

His shoes were full of sand. He pulled them off and clapped the heels together over the back porch and tossed them in the corner.

Maybe he'd wait till tomorrow to show Margaret the messed-up invitations. After a day like today he wasn't up for any complaining about something so minor, not from Margaret and especially not from himself. And he knew he *would* complain about them if given the chance. He'd whine and make himself believe it was important, and that would be a disservice to Stephanie—or at least to the image of her chasing after that stupid dog. Experiences like that were easily spoiled.

That night in bed Margaret said, "So you took her to the beach today." She was looking at a picture book of abstract painters her mother had brought back from New York. She was naked, the sheet spread across her legs, her fingers touching the painting, moving over the odd colors and angles.

"Yeah," he said. "Something different."

"Yeah," she said. "Tell me more."

He thought of telling her about the dog—he smiled, remembering—but he didn't know where to start. He said, "What is that supposed to be?"

"I don't know. A bicycle? A woman with a bicycle?"

He leaned to look at the reproduction over her shoulder. It did look like a woman with a bicycle, but it could have been a hundred other things as well. It was pretty good, the mix of yellow and black and the thin, nervous line work. "The more I look at it, the more I like it," he said and pumped his hips, and she laughed. He laughed too and pushed against her.

"Oh, yeah," she said. "The more I look, the more I like." She pushed her head down into the book like it was a pillow. She was giggling and kicking her feet, playacting but serious too. He loved how these moments happened—almost accidentally—and the trick was to stay in them, occupy them as completely as possible, and see them through to the end. He thought of the dog again, moving through the surf, the points of wet fur on its belly that Stephanie had called so punk rock.

"It was easier when you first started this," Margaret said, suddenly serious, as if she could read what he was thinking. "I thought I knew what it was about. I thought I knew the reasons for it. But it keeps getting more complicated."

He put his hand flat on her belly and told her he loved her. "I know," she said. "You don't have to tell me that right now. That's not what this is about, is it? If it is, then that's a different conversation."

The moment had ended, and they were in a new place, with different rules. How they had arrived there he wasn't quite sure, but it was a place he was getting familiar with. He folded his pillow in half and pushed it under his head, turning to the wall — a theatrical gesture, to be sure — and then he was asleep and it was morning and he was alone.

In the darkroom he put close-ups of Stephanie together in four rows of five. The phone rang, then stopped, then rang again. An hour later he went up to check if the caller, probably Stephanie, had left a message, and he caught himself locking the darkroom door.

When had he started doing that?

There was a kind of power in making mistakes, in shattering your life with your own hands and then living down deep in the rubble. In a way it was a kind of control, and Stephanie flaunted it like somebody else might flaunt wealth.

The first time they spoke, on a weekday in July when Jonathan was playing hooky from work, she told him, "I'm not so crazy about my tits. They're too small. Do you think they're too small?" Her voice was teasing, but mostly she seemed to be speaking honestly and inviting him to do the same.

"I guess," he said and wanted to share one of his own defects with her as a kind of balance.

"Do you want to touch them anyway?" she asked, but there was no invitation in it. If anything it was a shove, a newspaper rolled up and brought down on his nose.

He had thought he recognized her in the food court eating egg rolls and reading a magazine and wondered if it was the same person he had seen at that Goodwill bin. She was reading a magazine, not reading it really, but flipping the pages, getting the general sense of it. Her hair was longer and darker, and before she had been much farther away. He couldn't be sure.

He sat a few tables over with his frozen yogurt and watched four teenage boys fooling around at the men's room door. They were smacking at each other with open hands, fake karate jabs and awkward spins that made them look the opposite of how they wanted to look.

"Hey, you," she said to him. "Do you have napkins over there?" She held up both hands to show how shiny slick they were with grease.

He pulled a few napkins from the dispenser and walked over to her. That's when she said the comment about her breasts — because he had been looking down at her. Did she think she knew him? Or was this her way of getting acquainted with guys?

"No," he said to her question. "No. That's okay." He couldn't help but laugh. They both looked at the boys and their bad karate moves.

She said, "I hate kids."

The boys were hitting with closed fists now, and a security guard was watching as their laughter grew rowdier.

He handed her the napkins. "Thanks," she said, wiping her hands on a napkin and balling it up.

While he stood finishing his yogurt, they talked about the mall. They had both walked up and down its length and found little to interest them. She began to share things with him. "There used to be a drive-in theater on this land. In the center of a big field with all these pine trees on the edges and this stand that sold corn dogs. My mother brought me there once. I used to think it was far away. It seemed like we had to travel all night to get there. I don't remember the movie, but I remember running up and down between the parked cars, looking at people, causing trouble and stuff."

"I didn't know that," he said.

"Well, it's true," she said. "This whole area was completely different. Man, I wish those kids would shut up. There's nothing more disgusting than a fifteen-year-old boy." She threw the end of her egg roll on the floor as if it were a cigar butt and said, "It was probably one of the nicest things she ever did for me."

"What?"

"Taking me to the drive-in. Aren't you listening?"

She stood and kept looking at the kids, and that's when the idea of the project occurred to him, because of the way she was staring, with her eyes narrowed, her jaw set, her mouth a hard line. A person could photograph a face like that and never get the same image twice.

The boys did not notice her, but if they had, that look would have made them nervous. If they had been turning the pages of a magazine and found that face, the stare would have held them.

"You know," he said as they walked down to the Sears at the far end of the mall, "I have this idea." And he told her, and she shook her head like it was a line she had heard a thousand times, told by better people than he. He had to laugh at that, and he said, "Fine. I don't know what I was thinking," but she was still walking with him. If anything the electricity between them had been notched up a few volts, and when he said, "I'm going this way," at the water fountain, she followed.

"There are those kids again," she said.

They were different kids, the same number, but a year or two younger. They wore the same kind of baseball caps, the same baggy black T-shirts, and were slumped against the wall near the video game emporium. One of them, overweight with bad acne, glanced at her and then back at his shoes, which was probably what did it. As she passed she said, "Look at the cute virgins," like they were panda bears in a zoo.

One of the kids said, "What?"

"You heard me, virgin," she said, and she blew him a kiss. The fat kid looked like he had been slapped, although it was the other kid who was her target now. "Your nose is running," she said. "Are you going to cry?"

They all looked each other over, and then the kids moved off into the arcade. "C'mon," Jonathan said. "Let's go," and he reached out to touch her, but she was already moving, so he followed her instead.

When they got outside, the day had grown blustery, and they broke into a quick walk across the parking lot, hair whipping around their heads. He was invigorated enough to give her advice. "We're not slaves of our history," he pronounced sagely. It sounded like something he had heard from the mouth of a teacher or an actor in a foreign movie, and he concentrated on locating his car in the distance, because if he turned he probably would have seen her smiling that smile she had flashed at the boys.

"You wouldn't believe what happened to me today," he told Margaret that night at dinner.

"You wouldn't believe what happened to me either," Margaret said. "Remember all that work I did on Friday night? They completely dropped the ball, and we lost the client. They thought it was a sure thing, so they highballed him, and everything went up in smoke." She stabbed a cherry tomato with her fork. "What happened to you?"

"I met an interesting person," he said. He had her phone number in his pocket, and her first name, and the first photograph—a shot of her in the parking lot, taken with the cheap camera he kept in his glove compartment. He would mail it to her as a gift, with the promise of more if she wanted, and then follow up with a phone call.

"Oh, yeah?" Margaret asked.

"Yeah, it's sort of a job thing," he said. "Remember that project I worked on a little bit last year? Taking photographs at the soup kitchen?"

"Yeah," she said with a smile, but he was sorry he had brought it up, because he had gone to the kitchen only twice, on two Sunday mornings, and he wanted Margaret to understand that this new thing was more serious.

"It's like that," he said, "but better."

"That's great. Some of those photos you took were excellent, Jonathan. The gentleman with the prosthetic arm. That one was really powerful."

He remembered that one too. He wondered what had happened to it and what had happened to the man, who had talked in broken English about how to make good pasta sauce—something better than what he had been eating with the spoon held awkwardly in his left hand. His accent seemed Slavic, but Jonathan hadn't asked where he was from.

"I liked that one too," he said as he grabbed a slice of cucumber between his fingers. When he was excited, he ate with his hands. Cutting out the middleman, he once called it when Margaret complained.

"Yeah," she said. "He had a really interesting face. There was something so serene about his expression. It looked like he was falling asleep."

He made a grunt of agreement. During these conversations about his art he felt as if anything were possible.

"It's not for a lot of money," he said.

"That doesn't matter so much. We've talked about that."

They bowed their heads and ate quickly, because they were hungry and it was late. The meal was simple and delicious—thinly sliced eggplant and tomato with onion and garlic over brown rice. Jonathan was becoming a good cook, and he took pleasure in setting the table, placing the folded cloth napkins under the forks, lighting the single candle. He often got home from work earlier than Margaret, and he liked to be standing by the stove as she entered.

There it was—Stephanie puckering her lips with eyes half closed, arm raised toward the camera in a mock Nazi *Heil*. It always made him nervous to see it. Then there was the one with her back to the camera as she put on her coat, her hands invisible in the sleeves. A close-up of her laughing. Another of her shoulder and neck. An off-center shot of her sitting with both hands on the table, one open, one closed. Jonathan knew her fist clutched a couple of Celexa tablets, but they were invisible to the camera. A casual viewer might think something was there but wouldn't know what. It could be the cigarette lighter from another picture, could be a button from her coat, could be change or a pocketknife, could be anything small enough to grip and maybe important enough to hide.

He was assembling the photos into a new order, although the logic hadn't revealed itself yet. He had decided chronology was a dead end. It misshaped her life, streamlined and neatened it, boxed it into an easy kind of sense. This new order would be more instinctive and poetic — and maybe more hopeful too.

If he looked at the photographs long enough in groups of a dozen or more, themes emerged from the clutter of lips and eyes and legs. But every idea that popped into his head was as good as another and all of them were mediocre. On days like this he felt powerless and a little angry. What had Stephanie called him once? Galahad or Lancelot. Which one was the virgin?

He hadn't planned to go by her place, but he had been in the neighborhood, and he had his camera with him, and he was worried about her. She had opened the door and smiled as if she expected him, although she was dressed in her bathrobe. He could see the curve of her breasts, the flowered trim of her white bra, and a new mark on her chest about the size of a baby's palm. He had wanted to grab her by the wrist and drag her out of that apartment and into a new life, any new life, to do something as simple and dramatic as saving her.

When he had gotten home he wanted to pile up every photograph he had taken over the last two months and carry them back up those narrow stairs and throw them at her feet and say, *No, you look.* But instead he had come down into the darkroom and pulled some of them from one of the file cabinets beside the washing machine. These pictures were from when the project first began, and although Stephanie looked confident, there was tentativeness in the way he had framed the shots.

He remembered the day he took them, the way she had sprayed Lysol around the living room when they first entered and then had ducked into the other room, where she changed into jeans and a white button-down shirt. There had been a cat there then. He saw evidence of it anyway, in the litter box and small dish of pellets by the refrigerator. He had no idea where it had gone.

Up until then he had taken shots of Stephanie only on the street, standing before storefronts, phone poles, fire hydrants. When he asked if he could see her apartment, she said sure, why not, it's just around the corner, but he had felt himself tense. He hadn't really thought it would go that far. It had been an impulse to a large degree to ask if he could take pictures of her. Funny how a stray thought could gain such force in a person's life.

He flipped back to the picture of her saluting the camera. The sloppiness of some of the shots reminded him of pictures he had taken in college ten years ago. He did a series of nude body parts that together made a whole person. Stupid stuff trying to mask his limitations and laziness, but it had been better than the black-and-white pictures of bare trees and derelict buildings everyone else was taking. The photographs had all been of a woman he had convinced himself he was in love with, a shy anorexic with peroxide hair and scuffed boots who sat in the back of philosophy class drawing cartoons in her ring binder.

When he broke up with her at the end of the semester, she referred to the series as "the time you cut me into pieces," as if it had been something he forced on her. She seemed to have grown out of her shyness in that brief conversation. He remembered her defiant stare as she told him that the photos were hers, not his. But in that moment he saw her as his creation—not just the images in the photographs, but *her*, this girl who demanded things from him and looked him right in the eyes. The photos somehow made her that way, proud and righteously angry, and of course he had made the photos. He had reached out to touch her, but her hand was already on the doorknob.

He wished he had those photographs now. He saw them as snapshots of himself as much as of her—baby pictures from when he was learning to walk as a photographer and to assert himself as a person. Half the reason he took them was to offend the other students in the class, and his father, who had always wanted him to be an electrical engineer. For that reason alone they had been important.

And they had provided a way of introducing himself to Margaret. She was in that class too and later had told him that she admired the guts it must have taken to bring them in, tacked off-kilter to that yellow poster board, each one bearing the name of the body part. They had been smoking outside the health services building, and she smiled at him and said, "You're the only person from that stupid class still taking pictures, I bet."

In fact he hadn't been taking any pictures at all. He hadn't been doing much of anything except barely paying attention in class and watching soap operas and sitcoms in the public lounge of his dormitory. He had just finished a counseling session with the school psychiatrist about what she called his depression and general withdrawal. She asked him—softly as if he might break down right in her musty office—about his mother's losing fight with cancer ten years before, and he answered that he had been pretty young when all that happened, and although he missed her as an abstraction—who wouldn't miss his mother, after all?—he had to admit he didn't really remember her very well. She wrote all this down in quick motions of her pen and then asked more questions. He tried to answer each one carefully, as if he were being interviewed for an important job.

When the conversation shifted to his father, Jonathan danced around the subject as gingerly as possible. What could he say about the old man anyway? His slide from perpetual anger to perpetual regret had been surprising at first, but Jonathan's strategy for dealing with him had not really changed much—stay out of his way, agree with everything he said, that kind of thing. Though he did not tell this to the polite old woman writing his life story down in a notebook. He told her he loved his father, which was actually pretty true, and that he wanted to make him proud, which was not quite as true. When the hour was over, Jonathan thanked her and left the office with a sense of real accomplishment. He felt almost lucky, and Margaret must have seen that confidence as he lit his cigarette. Maybe that was why she spoke to him.

He assumed she was there to see the counselor too—and he instantly liked that common element between them—but he found out later she was just getting a flu shot. He said, "Yes, I've been taking a few pictures. Not enough though. But I have a lot of ideas." Which was true. His head was full of ideas. A *pollution of ideas*, he considered telling her but stopped himself.

They had gone out together that night and talked about his photographs and paintings and a half-baked sketch he had for a screenplay about how the school suppressed individual expression and freethinking. They talked about how miserable he was lately, and Margaret told him that a lot of creative people were melancholy and she could respect that even if his father couldn't. Her parents were no better. They confused morality with obedience, which she guessed was a disease that came with privilege.

"It's nice that somebody around here knows his own mind," she said.

Listening to her talk had cured something that was ailing him, and possibly he had done the same for her. Later he would tell her how angry he could get at the people around there with their BMWs and hand-knit cashmere sweaters, how sometimes their existence—their beauty and happiness paid for by Mom and Dad—seemed a personal affront to him. He would mention his scholarship—trying hard to sound as if he didn't care if he lost it—and then balance that information with details about his depression. He would tell her about the time he made shallow cuts across his wrists with a razor blade and the time—it was last semester but it seemed ages ago—that he swallowed an entire bottle of aspirin. He would tell her that his mother was dead and his father didn't understand him—nobody seemed to understand him—and that sometimes life seemed, well, dreary, didn't it?

"Guess how much my father makes a year?" she had asked at a party where they bumped into each other.

They walked to the algae-flecked pond behind the library to look at the ducks. She was drinking from a beer bottle. That's what you did at this school on weekends if you had a bit of the romantic in you. You got drunk and went to look at the ducks.

"What?" he asked.

"Guess how much my father makes a year?" she said again.

It wasn't a boast. There was irony there, but he had learned that irony was everywhere in a life reared on private schools and riding lessons. So the irony didn't surprise him. But her hint of contempt did. "I don't know," he said. "How much?"

"Guess."

"I don't know," he said. He hoped this game didn't have a second stage in which she was required to guess how much his father made.

"You have to guess."

"I don't even know what he does for a living."

"He's in marketing," she said. "He's worked on some very big ad campaigns. You know that thing with the talking dog? He did that."

Ah, some pride was there after all. She turned and smiled at him and tilted the beer to her mouth. They walked to the pond and looked around for the ducks. A patch of them drifted on the other side, lit up by moonlight.

She had slurred the word *campaigns*. She had slurred the word *dog*. He smiled to hear her speak. The last time he talked to his father on the phone he had told him that he was doing better in his classes and that he had met a nice girl. He was surprised to realize that the imaginary girl he had told his father about was not that different from this person here, although the other one hadn't been drunk.

Margaret had crouched down and looked out across the lake and hushed him, although he wasn't saying anything. She watched the ducks swim in small circles, and he looked at her watching the ducks, and he suddenly had a longing to see them through her eyes. Her expression was that sublime and tender. She had a little bit of the hunter in her crouch, as if she might lift a rifle to her shoulder, but her face—well, he wanted to kiss her. He walked over and crouched next to her.

"Anyway," she said, "how much?" The contempt had left her voice. Just a game now.

He thought of his own father, one of three employees for a small TV repair business, and realized the contempt had traveled to him. "A million dollars," he said.

Her laugh was quick and mocking, and for a second he thought it signaled the end of the evening, but she took his hand and stood up and looked around for her bottle. She had set it down in the grass. He bent down and picked it up and handed it to her.

"Close," she said. "Close." They began to walk around the pond. He wondered if drinking was a problem for her or if she had even more expensive vices. Someone from her background could acquire these as casually as another person might learn to pick her nose. He decided that was too harsh and put the thought aside. In its place he put another—that she had intelligent eyes.

"You know, I'm not one of these people who's impressed by money," he said.

"I know," she said with a laugh. "You're an artist."

"I'm not an artist," he said. "I just don't care."

His father had taught him to snake wire up through the walls of old houses. They had knelt together when he was ten years old and installed wall outlets around the baseboard of their kitchen. He hadn't known if that kind of experience made him susceptible or immune to the lives of most of the affluent students. He just knew that this girl was confident in a way he wasn't and that she was drunk and that he wanted to kiss her more with each passing second. He wanted to tell her about the aspirin and the razor blades. He would offer the stories to her carefully, like fragile gifts. He would run his hands up and down her body.

"What happened to those pictures from class?" she asked.

He had thrown them away, but if they went up to his room he would get his camera.

"We have to find Magnet," Stephanie said when Jonathan picked up the phone on a Sunday. More than two weeks had passed since their walk on Salisbury Beach, and at first he didn't recognize the name.

"What?" he said.

He was breathing hard from doing sit-ups, and she was breathing hard too. It was ten in the morning. He wondered if she had been to bed yet.

"The dog," she said.

"Oh," he said. "What about it?" He reached over and grabbed his T-shirt and wiped his chest with it. "Stephanie," he said, "tell me what's the matter. Are you okay? What did you take?"

"I didn't take anything," she said. "I had one drink and a Quaalude."

"Go lie down," he said. "Drink a glass of water and lie down."

"Jonathan," she said, "I really need your help."

"I'm with Margaret," he said, which was half true. She was downstairs on the couch, reading the Sunday *New York Times*. Later they might go out for coffee and take the paper with them. At noon they were meeting friends at their new condo and then who knew? The day would unravel like string.

"Goddamn it, Jonathan. I really need your help. I'm afraid that something horrible has happened."

"That was her, wasn't it?" Margaret said, when he came downstairs in his shoes and a wrinkled shirt.

"It shouldn't take long," he said as he fastened the buttons.

"I know," she said. "Is she okay?" But her voice didn't have much interest in it.

"I think so," he said.

"Okay," she said.

"Look. I don't know what to tell you. She's upset. She needs somebody. It's not like we had big plans. And there's a chance I might get some great shots. I should go. I'm sorry."

"It's fine with me," she said and pulled her head down behind the paper.

"Jesus," he said and made a show of rolling his eyes before swinging open the door.

So he and Stephanie drove along the boulevard in a lazy circle, two times, then three, then four. "We're not going to find it," he said.

"I'm such an idiot. I should have taken it when I had the chance. Poor thing. But I was worried. My landlady doesn't let me have pets. I used to have a cat, but she almost kicked me out because of it. It broke my heart to give that stupid little thing away. It broke my heart." She gave the dashboard a kick. "I'm serious. Do you have a cigarette?"

"Of course not," he said.

"Of course not," she mimicked. She smelled of peppermint and Marlboros, and there was a prizefighter cut on the bridge of her nose.

"Your landlady doesn't want you to have a cat, but she's fine with you letting those two crackheads in there, huh? That's peachy keen."

"Sarcasm isn't something you should fucking do, Jonny," she said. "You should leave that to the professionals."

"Like you?" he said.

"There it is," she said.

"That doesn't look anything like it, Stephanie."

But maybe it was. This dog was thinner and its hair was matted, but it had the same look to it, the same ears, the same low gait. He had seen only a glimpse of it. "Don't you tell me that miracles don't happen, Mr. Cameraman," she said in a kind of nervous elation. "Don't you tell me that." She was rolling down the window. "Hey, Magnet," she yelled. "Come here, boy. Come here. Come here, puppy. Come to Mommy."

A tattooed guy in a white T-shirt stood at the fried dough stand. He looked her way and grinned and yelled something back. Jonathan turned, both hands on the wheel, and headed down the dead-end street where the dog had trotted, trying not to look over at Stephanie, who was yelling, "Hey, boy, boy, boy. Come here, you pup-pup. You little monster."

He put the car into park, and with his left hand still on the wheel he said, "I think it's gone. Do you want to eat something? We should both have some food."

"Stupid dog," she said. "Go up there. There's a road over there."

"No," he said. He realized that he had forgotten his camera. There was the one in the glove compartment, but that was hardly better than nothing. He squeezed the wheel, and in his mind's eye he saw the two other cameras on the kitchen table where he had forgotten them, and then Margaret picking one up, clicking it on, adjusting the zoom lens. He reached across Stephanie and popped open the glove compartment. "Let's walk."

"I don't want to walk," she said.

"Fine," he said. "You stay here."

He fumbled out of the car and stood waiting for her, but she sat without looking at him, so he began to walk, deciding that any second she would catch up with him. He moved up the road at almost a run, past a goth couple holding hands. They had probably heard Stephanie yelling, although he doubted they connected him to the ruckus. He was wearing a clean, if wrinkled, button-down shirt and holding a camera after all. He stopped and smiled and snapped their picture beneath a Go-Carts sign. And without exchanging a word, he felt connected to them. He liked the boy's deep-set eyes and the girl's slumped shoulders, her pierced lip and eyebrow. He could imagine them years later talking about this. Maybe it was their first date, and he was a small part of it. "Have you seen a dog?" he wanted to ask them, but that would have put a fissure in the perfect moment.

He took two pictures up the street of breakers crashing against the rocky beach, although he knew from the quality of light that they wouldn't be worth the ten seconds it took to snap them. Then he stood on a cement retaining wall and looked up the road at an expensive house that overlooked the ocean. Four large pillars rose from the sea into one end of it, where three walls of tall windows gave the owner a panoramic view of the sea. The house jutted above the water like the prow of a ship, and he wished Stephanie were there to make fun of it, but she was back at the car, sifting through his things.

What would she find? There was change mixed with paper clips in the compartment below the emergency brake. There were maps of Boston and Providence and Maine and Vermont. There was a flashlight with low batteries, some out-of-date coupons, and a two-year-old letter from his father. He remembered the letter with an odd kind of revulsion, and for a moment he thought of jogging back to the car.

The letter had been written a few days after his father had suffered the first of his two mild heart attacks, and the handwriting was small and scratchy like it had been written by a different hand. His father had not been the kind of man to write letters, but this one was thoughtful and articulate. The gist of it was: come visit me and we can watch baseball together. A game had been on as he wrote the invitation, and occasionally it digressed from whatever point it was making to report on the state of the game. Someone had been thrown out trying to steal second and it hadn't even been close, and the grass was green and lush at Fenway Park, and one of the problems with hospitals was that the color green seemed to be absent from almost everything but the food.

Jonathan took a couple more pictures and then decided that he had waited long enough. He had punished her enough. The word *punished* occurred to him with sudden force, and he realized what he had been doing, so he turned and headed back by a different street, past the darkened video game parlor and the little seafood restaurant with its folded umbrellas and plastic lawn furniture. The waitress was cleaning up from lunch, tipping chairs upside down on the tables inside. When he passed her, they nodded hello.

He still had enough time and nervous energy to snap some pictures of Stephanie on the beach or maybe standing in front of various closed-down businesses. Those could be good, although they might convey the wrong impression. She did not come here by herself. He remembered her saying last time that she hadn't stepped on the beach since she was a teenager.

He was thinking of her as a teenager—the sullen expression, the tense curve of her back as she lit a cigarette—when he got to where the car should have been. But it wasn't where he remembered it, and his hand touched his keys in his pocket, because for a second he thought he might have left them in the ignition. Then he saw the car parked farther down the street and knew he had just misremembered. It was facing the opposite direction on the opposite side of the street near a similar storefront.

The light inside the car was on, but not long enough to run the battery down, thank God. He turned the key and the engine started right up. The glove compartment was open, and a map had been unfolded and then folded again, badly, and left on the seat. She had probably been trying to pass the time, tracing blue lines to places with interesting names. He had played games like that as a kid on long car trips. It probably hadn't taken her long to get fed up and head off somewhere. He refolded the map but didn't come up with a much better result, so he stuffed it into a garbage can a few parking spaces down as he walked along the street. Maybe she was hanging out with the kids. He wandered around looking for her another ten minutes before deciding to head home.

That night in bed he told Margaret, "I think I'm going to pull the plug on it."

"On what?" she asked, and she slid a torn envelope, from the phone bill it looked like, into her book. He noticed that she had written a short list of addresses down the envelope. He recognized the names of friends Margaret had not seen in a long time.

"You know what I mean," he said.

"You should keep at it," she told him.

She was probably thinking that he did not have the stamina to stick with anything until it was finished. It was an uncharitable thought—not her judging him that way, but his supposing that she might—and he tried to make up for it by asking her what she was reading and then asking her if she was enjoying it. The only charity he had lately was for Stephanie.

And that wasn't true either. "I'm not helping her," he said.

"You're not supposed to be helping her, Jon. You're supposed to be taking pictures of her."

They performed their little competition for the lion's share of the blanket. "I think I identify with her," he finally said. No reply. After a few seconds he added, "We both had difficult childhoods."

He could hear the ticking of the watch still on his wrist, and he took it off and placed it on the nightstand. Then he turned off the light, and the room darkened except for the streetlight against the shade. He had decided she was asleep when she said, "You didn't have that difficult a childhood. What's with this difficult childhood thing all of a sudden?"

He thought maybe he should let her think he was asleep, but instead he replied, "You don't know. Trust me on that. You don't know the half of it," and she made a flirtatious humming sound. It was like they had just finished dinner in a good restaurant, and she was anticipating something delicious and fattening to finish up the evening.

"Ooh, secrets," she said.

He gave her his best poker-faced stare. Even though she couldn't see it in the dark, he wanted her to feel it, and to feel the force of his past, of Stephanie's past, which suddenly seemed linked to his own.

Stephanie had told him so many things. He wondered which ones were the lies.

In early September the school buses began driving up their street again on their way to the middle school on the next block. There was a chill in the air, and the kids were dressed in brightly colored coats and hats. Some of them walked in small groups, shuffling along slowly, sometimes halfheartedly smacking at each other. Jonathan's father pointed out one of them from the window—a boy holding a scarf folded in half like a sling, backpedaling, wisecracking, then turning and breaking into a run. "He reminds me of you as a kid," he said, and his laugh turned into a cough. "Man, oh man, I can never fly without getting a cold."

His father was visiting from Florida for the long weekend. That night they would meet Margaret's parents for dinner at a Japanese restaurant in Boston. He imagined the moment when the two men would greet each other—his father resting his weight on his cane, the light grip of their hands, a smile and a joke and then the pulling back of chairs from the table. "Ever eat in a place like this?" Margaret's father would ask. "No? Well, you're in for a real treat. And it's good for you too." Then they would talk about the few things they had in common—traffic and weather and the coming wedding.

The cell phone buzzed from the arm of the couch. "I'm in Connecticut, Jon," Margaret's father explained when Jonathan said hello. "I have some things I need to do here, but as soon as I tie up the loose ends I'll put foot to floor, and we'll be up there before you know it. And I'm bringing my appetite so be prepared."

"Okay," Jonathan said. "That's fine," but the line had already gone dead. He looked at the cell phone in his hand and realized it was one he had never seen before—shiny blue plastic like a toy in his palm. He wondered what happened to the old one.

"Good," his father said when Jonathan told him they would be eating later than expected. "You'll have time to give me that tour of the darkroom I've been begging for." He moved from the window toward the cellar, the rubber tip of the cane thumping against the carpet.

"I don't think I can give you a tour really. It's just a room. It's like giving a tour of a closet." But he opened the door for his father and led him down, his hand on his shoulder. The heel of his left foot made a horselike clomping as it fell on each stair. He wondered if his father was keeping up his exercises.

"Who's this?" the older man asked when he looked down at the latest pictures scattered on the table. Most of them were formal portraitures, except in some she was making funny faces—curling her lip Elvis style, sticking out her tongue, closing both eyes tight as if tasting something sour.

"This woman I'm taking some shots of," Jonathan said.

"Well, they're very good," his father said, and Jonathan suddenly felt the way he had when they first walked around the college campus years before, identifying the buildings, saying hello to strangers they passed on the narrow footpaths. The most wince-inducing moment had been in the cafeteria lunch line, when his father had shared information about his son's scholarship to anyone within earshot. Jonathan wondered if he was in for a similar experience at dinner.

"Let's not talk about this tonight," he said.

His father had found one of the naked ones—Stephanie's face in shadow, one hand raised in a fist, one breast clearly visible. He turned it right side up on the table and pursed his lips. "She looks mad about something," he said, and he turned it around again and moved on to the next one. "I'm not sure about Japanese food," he said. "Can I get something mild there? Maybe chicken soup or something?"

"We'll find something you'll like."

"I promise not to embarrass you," he said, and he smiled. "I like this one. It's more melancholy than the others. It's a good contrast."

"Yeah. That's pretty good. That was dumb luck, the way

that's lit. There are a lot of happy accidents when you're doing something like this."

"Who is she anyway?" his father asked, and his voice had changed, grown weary, heavy, as if the walk down the stairs had exhausted him. He had stopped smiling, and when he rubbed the back of his hand against his eye, he opened his mouth and a small choked sound came out. His other hand gripped the edge of the table, and for a second Jonathan thought he might fall. "What does she get out of this, Jon? What do you get out of this?" He was crying—or his eyes were watering at least—and one hand was shaking. "What are you looking for? I don't understand. You've got a chance at happiness. We're going out to dinner with your future in-laws in an hour. And then you show me this."

Jonathan lowered his voice to almost a whisper. "I didn't want to show you, Dad. You insisted."

"I didn't know. How was I supposed to know?"

"Oh, please. It's not like you've lived in some white castle your whole life. What did you think I was doing?"

He bowed and nodded his head and turned away from the table. "You're right," he said. "You're right. You're right."

Jonathan could hear Margaret running the vacuum upstairs.

That night at dinner Margaret's father paid for everything, of course, with a small secretive motion to the waitress and then the knifelike thrust of his credit card. His own father was telling stories about his time in Korea, leaning back, one hand on his water glass. How many times had he heard these stories? They changed over time and their message was refined or possibly lost altogether, as in the case of the one he was telling now, which seemed to be wandering around looking for a point. He was having a good time though.

A round of delicate Japanese beer in thin bottles appeared, and the plates were taken away. As Jonathan's father poured himself half a glass he turned to Margaret's mother, "You should see the photographs Jon's been taking, Jessica. It's very interesting."

"Tell us about it, Jon," Margaret's father said. "I've been curious about what you've been doing lately."

"It's really something," Margaret interjected, "but it's bad luck to talk about this stuff before it's finished. He might jinx it."

Jonathan sent her a silent thank-you in his mind. The waitress returned with the bill and placed it at the head of the table.

"Everything was wonderful," Margaret's mother said, and his father nodded agreement, as if *they* were the couple. Jonathan had vivid childhood memories of his father in crowded restaurants. He would yell at the waitress, then at his wife when she tried to sneak some extra money into the tip, and then on the way home he'd rant about how the cook had probably spat in their food. But here he was, compliant, almost meek. He really did seem to be having a good time.

Margaret's father looked down and ran his hand across his head, smoothing his slicked-back hair. A stray lock fell across his forehead. "I wanted to give you some advice, Jonathan," he said, as he looked at the tablecloth, "but I'm not sure how to put it into words. I apologize if this doesn't come out quite right."

"That's okay," Jonathan said. "Go ahead."

"Well, Jonathan," he said, "this is what I believe. I don't believe in a lot, but when I believe in something, I really believe in it. Do you understand what I mean?"

"Of course," Jonathan said, realizing he felt the same way.

Someone was laughing at another table. Margaret's father looked over his shoulder, then at Jonathan. "You know," he said, "we're not much alike, I know that, but we have this one thing." He glanced over at Margaret and she smiled. Then he added, "The domestic life is a sweet life. I believe that, Jonathan. But a person has to give up his ego to make it work."

"I would agree with that," Jonathan's father said, and Jonathan felt vaguely ill. Then they all stood up, slipping on their coats, digging around in their pockets. There was a short discussion about who should drop off Jonathan's father at the hotel. "It'll give us a chance to talk more," Margaret's mother insisted, so Margaret and Jonathan finally excused themselves.

It was raining outside, and they stood under the awning talking. "He hates to drive in the rain," he said, "and your dad drives too fast. They're going to have a good time together." Jonathan took Margaret's hand, and they ran across the street to their car.

"He could have stayed with us," she said as they stood on opposite sides of the car. He beeped open the doors and they climbed inside.

"We paid for his hotel," he said. "I bet he's never stayed in such a nice place."

She made a noise of reluctant agreement and he started the car.

"You showed him the pictures?" she said as she pulled her seatbelt across her chest.

"Yeah," he said. "He insisted." He had not shown her any in weeks.

In bed she asked him, "Whatever happened to those pictures you took of me?"

"They're in the bureau where they've always been. Remember?"

"Not the last couple of rolls," she said, and then, "I thought the series of her in the sweatpants smoking was good. The composition had a lot of depth to it. Have you done more of that kind of thing?"

"No," he said.

"Your father never mentions your mother," she finally said.

"Yeah, well, it's been almost twenty years. He's over it."

Her voice seemed far away. She could have been talking from the next room. He decided not to look at her, to pretend she *was* in the next room. "I've been around widows before," she continued. "No widowers, but widows, and they'll mention their husbands at least a couple of times, especially when they're telling stories the way your dad was tonight. Do you think it's a gender thing?"

Sometimes she could take a point and pick and pick and pick. It's probably what made her so good at her job, but he wanted to tell her that it wasn't something she should bring to bed. "It's not a gender thing," he said. "It's not even a thing. It's nothing. It's been two decades, and they didn't even love each other in the first place." He hadn't meant to say that. But was she even listening anymore? He thought of his father riding to the hotel that night, watching the rain bead up on the windshield, one shaky hand on the dash. "Are you crying?" he asked.

"Yeah," she said.

He squeezed her hand and said, "It's okay."

"Oh, I know," she said. She sniffled and laughed in the dark like they had just watched a sad movie and now it was over, and wasn't it funny how she had cried at such a stupid story?

When they had first met, he suddenly remembered, he had taken pictures of her in baggy sweaters, naked from the waist down, pictures she said she wanted to mail to her parents with a note saying, *Hello, I'm doing well, how are you?* She said, "You need to kiss me."

"Then I'll kiss you," he said, but he didn't.

"Okay. Don't stop."

"I won't."

She said, "Good."

In their early days those photographs had been a way to make their relationship more real. Maybe that's what he was doing with Stephanie. He was making her life more real. Or not. Maybe it was just the reverse—that with each photograph of her he was the one becoming more substantial. He could measure himself by the photos of her thighs, the close-ups of her faraway looks. He was there, hidden in her eyes and in the placement of the frame around her nipple or mouth and in the hope that she might be more than this, more than a bunch of photographs of a part-time prostitute and drug addict in Lawrence, Massachusetts.

He wanted to capture her, lay her bare on film or some not so pretentious sounding equivalent. But he also wanted her to escape—escape the pull of her apartment and life and in an odd way escape *him*—because maybe the project's failure meant her success. To some degree he knew he was documenting her desperation, her slide into some nameless place that, if it wasn't death, was its sister in obscurity, its lack of possibilities. There was a strange sense that when the project ended she would cease to exist. Or that *he* would cease to exist, which was ridiculous but somehow plausible.

Whenever he saw his father, Jonathan was reminded of the

suicide attempts of his teen years, those stupid little cries for help, the shallow baby cuts on his wrists, the awkward, sentimental note that was supposed to contain his last words. His mother had been dead several years by then, and the idea of leaving his father alone in the house had seemed like the kind of magnificent, ironic punishment a nineteenth-century novelist might think up. It was a surprise for Jonathan to discover how much he wanted to live, another surprise when his father reacted with such gentleness and fear. He remembered him touching the back of his hand—not the bandaged wrist but the hand—and crying in much the same way he had cried that afternoon.

"He changed after she died," he said, still imagining that Margaret was in the other room, that he was by himself. "It was like he shrank. His voice too. You should have heard the way he used to yell."

"You have to forgive him someday," she said.

"I forgave him years ago," he said, and then when she didn't answer, "Forgive him for what?"

Still nothing.

"It's not that easy to forgive somebody," he said as he pushed his pillow into the right shape. "Aren't some things unforgivable?"

"You tell me," she said, which was worse than not saying anything, because it demanded a complicated response. He decided not to give her one. He twisted his back to her and stared at the wall.

Jonathan was glad his father had seen the pictures. He wished only that they were better. In a way that was what he owed Stephanie.

Art was superstition, because it involved faith in the unknown.

And love was superstition for the same reason. Sometimes it was difficult to tell the difference between the two, especially when he was developing film, watching a picture take shape in the tray of Dektol, before the fiber paper had been washed with fix and washed again with fix remover, before the picture had realized its possibilities as an image and you were looking at the next one. In that suspended moment the photograph could be anything because it was nothing, and was there anything as lovely as the perfect photograph that hadn't happened yet but just *might?*

Maybe this was how Margaret saw him. He did not understand how she could love him otherwise. It must have been the way his parents saw him as a child, and it was the way his father would talk about him at the wedding, which was really why Jonathan cringed when the subject of his photography had come up at dinner and why he squeezed Margaret's hand again and slid out of bed and down to the darkroom.

He took a good third of his photographs from the file cabinet near the washing machine—all two hundred something of them—and spread them across the heavy table and hoped they would tell him something new. But the only thing they ever told him was that he needed to take more.

"Are you asleep?" he asked when he finally came back to bed.

"Yes," she said.

"Me too."

After that second trip to Salisbury Beach, he and Stephanie did not go there again, although she talked about it the way she sometimes talked about Florida—as a place so perfect it bordered on the imaginary. Sometimes when talking she slipped back and forth between the two—the impending trip to Florida, the beach trip already taken—so that it was difficult for him to sort them out.

His father asked about her once in late February during one of their short phone conversations. "How is that girl doing?" he asked.

"Who?"

"The girl in the photographs. Is she okay?"

Margaret passed by and touched him on the shoulder, and he smiled, then turned his attention back to his father.

"Yeah. She's okay." He had seen her two days before and shot a couple of rolls he felt especially good about.

"I think I've got it figured out," he said. "You know—what's going on with you two."

"No theories," he said. "Please."

"It's not a theory," he said. "It's just an opinion."

Jonathan wondered how far he could push him before his old anger rose up in defense, but he said, "Margaret's calling me. I have to go."

"What's up with him?" Margaret asked when he walked into the other room. She was drinking tea on the sofa, legs curled underneath her.

"Nothing much," he said and sat down next to her, looking at the magazine she was reading. He vaguely registered a large picture of a lush greenhouse, a smaller picture of a smiling couple on the opposite page.

"What were you talking about?" she asked.

"The wedding," he said.

"So he didn't tell you his theory?"

"What?"

"His theory about you and Stephanie," she said with a small smile. "He told me about it last week."

He noted that Margaret had used the same word he had. *Theory.* It made him feel closer to her somehow, but he still didn't want to hear about it. He took her tea from her hands, set it on the coffee table, put his hands on her knees, and said, "She's messed up. But she's okay. And I honestly think she's getting better."

"Do you sometimes talk about those things?" she asked.

Playing ignorant he said, "What things?"

"You know," she said. "Your history."

"New rule," he said. "You and my father don't talk about me. How does that sound?" He lifted his arms in an open gesture. *Just shoot me in the heart.*

"You know, we're not that different from one another," he told Stephanie that night.

"Definitely," she said. They were standing on her stairs, and she had a beer bottle with a torn label in her hand. "You're saying that because you think I'm mad at you about deserting me at the beach. But I'm not. Don't sweat it, man. I didn't even wait around for you. I got a ride and I got something else too, so no sweat. It's not like I need you or anything."

"You're angry," he said. "You don't know you are, but you are." That was *his* theory anyway.

"Nope," she said and opened the door wide for him.

There was the dog. Or rather *a* dog. She said, "Magnet, this is my boyfriend. Boyfriend, this is Magnet. I hope you two get along."

The dog pushed its face against his thigh, and he ran his hand through the matted hair on its head. One of its eyes was discolored with pinkish blood. He crouched and took its head in his hands and thought about telling her that this wasn't the same dog they had seen the first time at the beach, but now that he was petting it he wasn't so sure, and what did it matter anyway? "Hey, Magnet," he said. "How are you doing? Is she treating you right? Driving you crazy yet?"

"I'm feeding him hamburgers," she said. "I'm treating him better than I treat myself." She was laughing so that her crooked teeth showed. "No pictures, though. None of that. I'm in too good of a mood."

"Sure," he said, as he rubbed the dog's belly. He realized that he was in a good mood too.

She said, "I thought I wasn't going to see you again. I thought you had decided to flush the whole project and take pictures of babies or something."

"I just wanted to give you a few days off," he said.

"She doesn't want you to see me."

He decided to let that stand.

"Bitch," she said, but she was smiling. She held out a joint like she expected him to light it, but he waved it away. "What do you mean we're alike?" she asked.

"I never said you are alike."

"No," she said. "Me and you. You said we're alike." There was irritation in her voice but also interest. She was in a mood to talk and even to listen.

So he said, "We're both self-destructive, you and I. A little bit."

"Oh, yeah?"

"We both have histories." He picked up a small chipped statue from her table, something he had not seen there before—one of the three wise men, the top of his skull gone and his face rubbed smooth to a blank. It was about the size of a chess piece. He placed it back on the table facing the other direction, toward the door, and told her, "There's a lot I could tell you."

"Like what?" she asked, although she seemed to be losing interest. Still he sat down and began to talk, his arms resting on his knees, slightly hunched forward. The apartment smelled different today, he decided. It was a clean smell, and he breathed deep to take it into his lungs.

"I wrote an essay years ago. In my freshman composition course. We were required to write a compare-contrast essay."

It was easy with someone like her. She moved around the room, picking up dirty glasses and pillows, and he closed his eyes and leaned back and said, "Mine was a comparison of my suicide attempts. Cutting versus pills. Leaving a note versus not leaving a note. Right down the line."

"How positively dark of you," she said, heading into the kitchen. "Did your teacher give you an A?" she called back.

"Nah," he said. "I never turned it in." Glasses clattered in the sink, and water began to run. "I never talk to my father about those times." He raised his voice but kept his eyes shut. "It's always in the background somewhere though."

She came back in, and he looked up at her. He wondered what she looked like when she was eight years old, if she had that cocky defiance even then, if she got in trouble for teasing the family pet or setting fires in the backyard. "You've never mentioned your father," he said.

"Not worth mentioning," she said.

He laughed a little too loud and leaned forward again. "My father changed after my mother passed away. I couldn't believe how meek he became." She made a sound of acknowledgment, so he continued. "Before that he was always storming around the house and slamming doors." He held up both hands to frame his face and puffed out his cheeks. "His face would get all red and crazy."

"Abusive," she said, like she was jumping to the conclusion she knew he was going to reach anyway in another ten minutes.

He had never thought of using that word, but it was interesting to consider.

"The invitations aren't right," Margaret said. She still had her coat on, and she was holding the box in both hands. It contained a couple hundred cards and envelopes that needed to be sent to uncles and aunts and cousins and friends of Margaret's parents and people she had known in college. Several would go to childhood friends of hers who now lived in places like Cincinnati and Saint Louis and Des Moines. Another was going to her old philosophy professor. It took this kind of formal exercise, sometimes, to make a person realize how few connections he had to the world. When it had come time to dredge up the names of his friends and family who should receive invitations, he had been able to come up with only twenty or so people, and half of them did not make the final cut.

"Just look at them," Margaret said.

He had forgotten to lock the door to the darkroom.

"I know," he said. "It's been a bad day."

"Well, you shouldn't have accepted them if you knew they weren't right. You paid for them?"

"On the credit card." It seemed ridiculous talking about such things, but everything could seem ridiculous after seeing Stephanie. He had snapped two rolls of her late that morning, but she had still been sleepy eyed and irritable. Up late the night before, partying or making a living. Jonathan had wondered if she could tell the difference.

Margaret was wearing her new leather coat with the zipper pulled down just above her navel, a tight ribbed black turtleneck, and probably one of her dark blue bras underneath. He thought of the birthmark on her right breast and how he sometimes kissed it as she fell asleep after they made love.

"We're taking them back," she said. "I think we should take them back right now."

"Sure," he said, "okay," and he looked around for his coat. "But we don't have to. They're on the credit card, after all." It was fine with him though. This seemed to be turning out as well as it could have, and maybe it would get late enough that they'd end up going out to eat, since he had spent the day with Stephanie or with pictures of her instead of making dinner. And anyway, the trip back would give Margaret a chance to cool off about his stupid mistake.

She came over and put her arms around him, her cheek on his shoulder. "I'm sorry to be such a stickler, Jonathan, but this is a once in a lifetime deal. It needs to be done right."

"I know." Her father was paying for the caterer, the hall, the cake, the dresses for the bridesmaids, just about everything. The invitations were a drop in the bucket. Still this meant certain compromises—a string of them, actually.

Jonathan had never been inside the country club where the reception would be held. Margaret and her father had handled that end of things. But from far away the estate looked as white and pristine and virginal as Margaret's wedding dress. Each weekend at least one party was held there celebrating something, whether it was a marriage or retirement or silver anniversary. The building was a monument to exactly the kind of thing Margaret's father had talked about the last time they had seen each other, but it was also a place, Jonathan knew, where old men got drunk on Thursday nights and mocked their wives—and their mistresses too. They fell asleep in large leather chairs with cigars burning in ashtrays as waiters brought coffee in small porcelain cups. He had no idea how much it cost to rent such a place, or to buy Margaret's wedding dress, or even to hire the priest. He assumed the priest wanted something, even if they called it an honorarium.

"Hey, are you okay?" Margaret asked. There was a hint of demand in her voice. Something bad had probably happened at work today, but he didn't really feel like listening. Maybe later when they were sitting in front of the television or curled in bed and their minds were operating closer to the same wavelength.

"I'm fine," he said.

"Are you sure?"

"I'm sure. I guess I just need to be more detail oriented."

That reminded Jonathan of the ad campaign her father had talked about the last time they had visited her family. He was a private consultant now and had recently planned a campaign for a high-end home furniture company. They manufactured small uncomfortable chairs and softly glowing table lamps of intricate design. *Because the details matter.* That was the tagline used in the catalog, the product of his imagination that had earned some of the big money he was now spending on a five-course meal for two hundred wedding guests.

They drove the long way to return the invitations because Margaret wanted to stop for some bread at the German bakery she liked so much. She left the engine running and went inside, and as Jonathan sat there tuning the radio from station to station he decided that the whole thing was plain stupid. There was no reason to return the invitations right now. Who cared what color the paper was? Who would know the difference?

Margaret's parents, that's who.

Jonathan turned the ignition off. He hated the way she wasted things—gas, energy, time. It was frivolous to leave a car running like that. Where was she anyway? He also hated the way she had to make everything perfect where her father was concerned. He had once taken Jonathan aside at a dinner party and said, "Nothing is too good for her, Jon," in a stilted way that made it seem like Jonathan should say something back. He was always doing that, wrapping an arm around Jonathan and leading him somewhere like the fireplace, leaning in close so that Jonathan could smell the Scotch on his breath—always Scotch—and then offering worldly advice and sage insights that often sounded like little more than catchy ad slogans. Like that time at dinner with Jonathan's father sitting right there nodding along.

Jonathan decided that the next time he saw Margaret's father he would simply ignore him as much as possible, but then he realized that the next time would be the wedding, which made him feel bad enough to reach over and start the car for Margaret as she stepped out of the bakery.

"Look at this," she said, handing him the bread. "Pumpernickel."

It was still warm. He loved to make sandwiches from warm bread—some thinly sliced roast beef, provolone cheese, a little pepper, that expensive mustard he was always telling himself he could do without. He cradled the loaf and felt the warmth on his lap and wondered if maybe they should swing by the deli in case they were out of the mustard at home.

"That bagel place went out of business," he said, and Margaret politely glanced to one side enough to register the pulled shades, the empty parking lot. He had noticed that earlier in the day when he had driven this same route going to and from Stephanie's, and it had made him acutely sad. The owners had been nice people. They had been doing a steady business. Something bad must have happened.

"What did you do today?" she asked.

"Errands," he said, then added, "picked up the invitations."

"Is that all?"

He wasn't unemployed, not really. He had taken what had admittedly been a bad accident—two bosses who couldn't mind their own business, that stupid pink slip coming at exactly the wrong time—and turned it into something that was his choice.

"Stephanie's talking about Disney World again," he said. Which was more than he had intended to say. It was as if he had somehow been tricked into it.

"Oh, yeah?" Margaret said. Hesitation had started coming into her voice whenever that name came up. It was a recent thing. Two days before, when he was in an especially bad mood, he had gone for a walk around the block, and by the time he was three houses away he had decided that Margaret was simply jealous. Although he knew it wasn't true, at the time the idea somehow made him feel hopeful, even inspired. Because if it was true that would mean Margaret's feelings for him were beyond her rational control. He liked that. Even now he liked it, and he thought about it with the same mix of apprehension and distaste he had felt so long ago when Margaret had told him about what her father did for a living and how her family was what she called comfortable.

He slid the heater switches up and down their grooves, then back to their original settings. He imagined her slipping out of her expensive coat, pulling her turtleneck off over her head, those two seconds when her belly became exposed and she was sightless.

He said, "She sounded awful."

"She asked you for money," Margaret said.

"No," he said, although for a second he wanted to say yes. Sometimes he had an urge to take out the worst parts of Stephanie and show them to Margaret—she said *this*, and she was wearing *that*, and *look at this one*. He didn't know why. It had taken him more than a month to show the first tentative nudes to Margaret, but when he did he had felt a rush of something resembling triumph.

They were moving around the rotary. Margaret turned off the radio and said, "You went by to see her. You said *she sounded awful*—that's exactly what you said—because you want me to think you talked to her on the phone."

She used the same glance on him now, the quick, decisive one she had used on the abandoned bagel shop a minute before. "Whether you're aware of it or not, that's what you wanted me to think, Jonathan." And she motioned for a car to go ahead, to move out in front of her. Then she fell in behind it, the small procession moving up to a red light. It was rush hour and the traffic was beginning to slow and stick. For some reason it annoyed him that she was so polite to the other car.

"Of course I went by there," he said. He felt a kind of righteous anger that seemed indistinguishable from the real thing, as if he really had been condemned unjustly. He'd had the idea for this project longer than he had even known Margaret, for Christ's sake. The germ of it anyway. Since he was in that stupid photography class. It could just as easily have been a phone conversation, he told himself. Stephanie called me. She was asking for a favor. She wanted me to drive her somewhere to score something. I told her no. But I couldn't leave it at that. I had to go see what kind of shape she was in.

"Listen," he said, "I *need* to do this. I need to do it *my way.*"

"I know. I like that you're doing it. I respect it. When I hear you working down in the cellar it makes me happy. It's just that sometimes I think you're in too deep."

"Yeah?" She had said this kind of thing before. She was probably right, but that didn't necessarily change anything. This kind of project seemed to necessitate getting in too deep. That was the *definition* of the project.

"Jonathan, one of the things that makes you special, that makes you unique, I think, is how innocent you are. I don't mean that to sound bad at all. But I worry about you."

She was probably thinking about some of the pictures she had seen, big men sitting around Stephanie's apartment, beer in one hand, cigarette in the other, hash pipe on the table, the amused expression of someone whose day had just become more interesting. *Sure you can take my picture. You want me to smile for you?*

"I know what you're thinking. You're wondering why I'm so afraid of you getting your hands dirty." She sighed and looked out her side window, then back at her hands resting on the steering wheel. "Maybe you're not in deep at all. But *she's* in deep, I know that much. Maybe that's what bothers me. Why do you want to do this anyway? I mean, why did you choose *this* subject?"

He could see that they were taking the first steps to some kind of calm reconciliation, but he didn't want that, not right now. He wanted to nurse the anger a little longer. Make Margaret see that his concern for Stephanie was right. So he decided to tell her something he had never told her before. He looked out the window at the car inching along next to them and said, "You're just jealous."

At first he thought she hadn't heard, but then she smiled and shook her head no. They were stuck in traffic, displayed fishlike in the aquarium of the car, and it was one of the few discreet gestures available to her. If they weren't stopped dead maybe she would have slammed on the brakes, done something more dramatic. Maybe she would have slapped him if they had complete privacy. He looked at her, as if he were measuring the space between them. He was in love with her—he really was—and he was acting like an idiot.

"You fucking pig," she said. It was the worst thing she'd ever said to him. It was like they were in a movie. The rest of the cars were the audience. The light turned green.

"I'm just tired," he said. "I've been working too hard. Doing this kind of thing, it colors your perceptions."

"You haven't been working at all, Jonathan. I get up every day, I'm at work by eight o'clock, and then I come back home, and I have to fix the mistakes you spend the day making. *That's* the kind of thing that'll color your perceptions."

Someone beeped from behind. Margaret stepped on the gas, and the car jerked forward.

He said, "It's just that I feel this sense of pressure. It's like everything is coming to a head. I mean, the next time I see your father he's going to ask me how the job is going, and what am I going to tell him?" He decided now that being fired—that's what it was; he was fired—was not the little triumph he had imagined. There was the wedding and after that an ever lengthening list of responsibilities. He needed to get organized, get his priorities straight. He had told himself these things before. He was sick of it, sick of himself. He was pretty sure Margaret was too. He sort of hoped she was.

"You know, you have a pretty narrow view of people. Do you really think my father cares that much about the little details of our lives? Do you think he has so little trust in me?"

"It's not a little detail."

"No, not right now. But it will be in a couple of months after you've been working at a new place for a while, and you're wondering about a promotion." She smiled. She had found another opening, a tender spot. "When you have a nice, comfortable office, and you're worrying about all the meetings you have that afternoon."

She was trying to paint a picture and put him in it, but try as he might he couldn't see himself in such a room, answering that phone, worrying those worries. He said, "I don't know about that."

"I do. I definitely know about that. That's what they call human nature." She grew quieter. "It's strange," she said, and her voice was an odd mixture of anger and puzzlement. "This just occurred to me. When we first met, one of the things I liked about you, about us, was how *separate* we seemed from everyone else."

"Yeah?"

"But now it's you and her against the world, isn't it, Jon?" And then something else, but he wasn't listening anymore.

It started almost as a joke. He put two fingers to his temple and clucked his tongue against the roof of his mouth.

"What are you doing?" she asked.

Russian roulette. He had done it before when stuck in traffic while commuting to his old job, during those last two weeks when he was bored and frustrated and looking for anything to pass the time. Just once or twice, enough for another driver to notice and wonder what was going on with that strange person holding his fingers to his head.

He pulled the pretend trigger and decided to make himself lucky this time. He spun the cylinder, clucked his tongue again—the hammer being pulled back—put his fingers in position. There was something newly satisfying about it.

"Is that supposed to be funny?"

He made the sound again. He put his fingers back. He wanted to hurt himself a little, more out of curiosity than anything else. He wondered what it would feel like, his mind splintering and melting away. But he also wanted to hurt her, and this was a simple way to do it, like a child parroting someone's words back to them. The repetition was the thing. The snap of the tongue. Fingers to the temple. Slight hesitation. He was lucky again.

"Stop it."

He didn't know what would happen if he kept pushing. It was as if he already saw the moment in retrospect down the deep tunnel of a year or two, looking back from some different place. This moment. It was important in its fragility. *Our lives together*, he thought, *this life*, meaning the two of them in their car, their house, their bed; it was something you could nudge out of position and then, who knows?

"Please stop it."

The thing was people from money landed on their feet. They might fall, yes, but they always had someone to catch them. That was a better way to put it. He thought of Stephanie in her apartment with the single lamp, that stupid damp-smelling rug, the color and texture of a tabby cat. He put his fingers to his head.

Margaret swerved to the curb and stopped the car. "Get the hell out."

He couldn't help but chuckle. "What are you talking about?"

"Get out," she screamed. It was enough to drive him from the car. He fumbled for the handle, opened the door, and stepped out. They stared at each other for a second—her hands on the wheel, his feet on the side of the road—and then he shut the door softly, as if they had planned to drop him off in front of Sanborn's Tire and Tread all along.

They kept looking at each other, and for a second he thought she was going to reach across the passenger seat and open the door again. Then she turned, slapped her blinker on, and drove off. He laughed when he realized he was still holding the loaf of pumpernickel. He put his fingers to his head and made a sound like a bomb. "Ka-boom," he said. "Ka-pow."

The ground was gritty with dirt and broken glass. He noticed strips of rubber from a blown tire and a child's toy, a broken and mud-stained plastic action figure. He walked into the parking lot and stood by the pay phone watching the cars go by until he decided what he wanted to do.

"I got this for you," he said. She smiled and mumbled something as she leaned her head back. She blew smoke at the ceiling.

He put the bread on the table, and she said, "Rashid and his brother were here. They sold me some good stuff." Her eyes lolled to one side and she snickered. He sat down and began to eat the bread, pulling it from the loaf in small chunks.

"Florida," he said.

"That's right," she said. "Two weeks." She made a peace sign.

"How are you going to get there?"

"Greyhound, I guess."

"How much does that cost?" he asked.

He had walked three or four miles to her apartment, along the trash-flecked factory road that ran parallel to the river. She had called out from the couch for him to come in, and he had walked into her living room. He had entered it differently than other times, he noted, with real humbleness.

"You're upset about something," she said.

"No," he said. "No, I'm not."

"Yes, you are," she said. "You're pissed off."

"No," he said, and he looked around for the dog. There was no sign of it or its plastic water dish. He said, "So how much does the bus cost?"

"I have no idea what a bus costs. How the fuck am I supposed to know what a Greyhound bus costs? A hundred dollars, okay? It's going to cost a hundred dollars. Two hundred dollars. Three hundred dollars. That's how much it costs. Three hundred dollars." She laughed and looked around for an ashtray. He had seen her in worse shape.

He said, "I have an idea."

"Of course you do," she said.

"Want to hear it?"

"No pictures today?" she asked.

Maybe because this was the first time he had been here without any camera at all, he was seeing her differently. She was not as beautifully desiccated as he had thought, as he had made her look in his favorite photographs of her. He wished he had even his simple Polaroid.

"Do you want to hear my idea or not?" He was determined to stick with his plan. He had thought a lot about this on his way over.

"Sure. Sure."

"I'll drive you to Orlando. For free. I'll drive you, and I'll take pictures, and it will be a way for me to finish up my project. It'll take what, three or four days or something?"

"Oh, yeah," she said. She looked over at her TV, which was off, but her eyes lingered there, watching an imaginary show.

"Yeah," he said.

"Yeah." Was she sleeping?

Her eyes pivoted toward him. She wasn't sleeping. She said, "I want to stay in nice hotels. I've never stayed in a nice hotel. One with a sauna." She smiled at him and closed her eyes and moaned like she was faking a mild orgasm, like she was hungry. "Separate beds though, you little fucker. Separate beds. Unless you don't want that." She stood up and approached him. "What do you want?" she asked. "Do you know what you want?"

He wanted to drive to Orlando with her. He wanted to take pictures of her as she made her escape, with the scenery of eight or nine different states as background. He wanted to turn to his right as he drove and see her there looking back at him.

"I want to help you," he said.

"Where's your camera?"

"Are you okay, Stephanie?"

"You lost your camera, didn't you? Rashid stole it. He took it right off your neck, and now he's going to sell it."

"I left it at home," he said.

"You brought bread instead," she said and snickered.

He bent down in front of her. "Are you okay, Stephanie?" he asked.

"Oh, sure. Sure I'm okay. We're going to Orlando. What kind of car is that thing you drive? A Volvo? A Volvo. You drive a Volvo. Jonathan drives a blue Volvo." She made the words into a children's song.

"Come on," he said with a little laugh. "Knock it off." His voice changed, grew deeper and more deliberate. He tried to be stern with her. He tried to look her dead in the eyes.

She looked back at him. "Oh, man," she said. "You really do want to go to Florida, don't you? You want to go more than I do." There was something bloody in the corner of her eye he had never noticed before. Or maybe it was new. It was splotchy and bright as a strawberry and seemed to press itself against the edge of her iris.

He said, "I'm just trying to help you."

She said, "So give me some money, and I'll take the bus. Give me two hundred dollars, and we can do whatever you want. We can do it here, or we can do it in your Volvo. Then I'm gone. I'm gone like a magic trick."

"I'm just trying to help you," he said and put his hands on her shoulders and shook her gently. He pushed her back and watched her expression change from smug satisfaction to shock and then to pleasure. He realized that this was the first time they had ever touched. There was a one-sided grin on her face as he dropped both his hands to his side. He leaned forward and so did she, tilting her head slightly, almost shyly. She touched his chest and said, "Okay. Come with me then. Let's run away together."

"Stop it," he said.

"Let's hit the road together. I'm serious now. Let's go."

He backed up. She stepped forward, put her hand against his chest again, and grasped his wrist with the other. They were almost dancing. "Let me go," he said.

"I thought you wanted to escape with me," she nearly yelled, her grip tighter.

"Stop."

"We can leave tonight."

"No," he said. "I can't."

Mock surprise. Mock anger. Her hand falling away from his chest. The other hand still holding him. "What?"

"I can't."

"But you're the one who just suggested it." Then she smiled and released him. "Pussy." The door was still ajar. He walked over to it. She followed him. "Hey," she said, "at least give me some money, right? Two hundred bucks should do it."

He pictured her climbing on board the bus with a dirty gym bag. "I don't have two hundred dollars," he said. He didn't know if he would have given it to her if he did. He was glad he didn't have to make the decision.

She said, "How much do you have?"

He had forty-five dollars. Two twenties and a five. He handed all of it over.

"Jesus," she said. "I don't know what you want me to do with that." She was smirking at him. "That won't get me far. I'll end up in New Hampshire and freeze to death." But she took it and folded it and stuffed it in her pocket.

He said, "The project isn't finished."

"Oh, Christ," she said. "Forget the project. You wouldn't have finished it anyway, and fuck, you know, nobody would care even if you did."

Why did this seem like something Margaret would say? It simply wasn't true. It occurred to him that Margaret might be more connected to Stephanie through their womanhood than he was connected to Stephanie through . . . what? Mutual pain? Hardship of the soul? "Listen," he said.

"No. No, I won't listen." She yelled and jerked her arms like a child throwing a temper tantrum, like a crazy person.

"Hey," he said. He moved to grab her wrists. They shifted around the room, she struggling halfheartedly, tugging and huffing and swearing—a ridiculous slow-motion dance. How did I get here, he wondered, to this strange moment, wrestling with a woman I hardly know in a place I don't want to be?

Her lips curled, and she said, "This would make a nice photograph, wouldn't it?"

Suddenly she was on the floor, one leg pulled to her stomach and hands outstretched, head bent to the dirty rug as if she were kissing it. He stood over her and realized he had pushed her.

He moved to help her. She flinched. He stopped and drew back. He turned to the door but then had to turn back to her. "I need money for a taxi."

She dug in her pocket and handed him a twenty.

"Where's the dog?" he asked.

"Oh, him," she said. "He was annoying. And he couldn't have made the trip. My sister doesn't like animals anyway."

"Yeah," he said, "I think you told me that once."

Stephanie's apartment was on the third floor of a run-down Victorian building. Once upon a time it had been a single dwelling, but it had been divided into five apartments, three in front, two in back. From one of the apartments in the rear came loud music and laughter.

Out on the street Jonathan looked for a taxi in the dark. Just when he began to think he'd have to walk all the way home, one finally came by. "Hey," the driver said after Jonathan got in, "you want to hear a funny joke?"

"Okay," Jonathan said. It was easier than saying no.

But the driver didn't say anything else. Maybe he hadn't heard. Jonathan looked out the window and let himself be carried home. He thought of Stephanie handing him the twenty-dollar bill, her fingers against the palm of his hand, the way she let her touch linger. He remembered the cuts on her knuckles and the pinky nail she sometimes nibbled when nervous, and he suddenly thought of her performing sex acts for food again, with the guys who worked second shift at the textile company. He had photographed them from the window—forlorn figures standing in the alley with their hands in the pockets of their overalls.

He imagined himself now as one of those men, wandering around the edges of the early morning, still buzzing from his coffee and not wanting go home to his children and to his wife, who was awake and waiting to hear his footsteps coming up the stairs.

The flawed invitations were on the counter where he usually left his wallet and keys. He crept into the bedroom, moving cautiously in the dark, and listened to Margaret breathe. He felt like he could listen to her all night and still be standing there in the morning when she woke.

He sat on the edge of the bed and swung his legs around. He would sleep on top of the sheets tonight. Although he wanted to say he was sorry, he knew it wouldn't be enough. Not tonight. His eyes were adjusting to the dark, and he turned on his side and watched her sleep. He leaned forward and kissed her lightly on the forehead.

When the alarm rang the next morning, he listened to Margaret pulling on her slacks, running the water in the bathroom, brushing her teeth. He stood up and pulled on his jeans.

He said, "Good morning."

She said, "I made coffee."

"Great," he said.

"I called in sick. I'm just not in the mood. Maybe I'll go in for a half-day later or something."

They looked at each other, and he tried to smile. He said, "Want to return the invitations today?"

"Okay," she said. "Let's get it over with."

The print shop was in a strip mall, a long rectangular building pretending to be four different buildings, which also consisted of a golf shop, a place that sold bicycles, and a gaudy video store. The storefront was boring and familiar, but seeing it was almost shocking because on the ride over Jonathan had forgotten about the world outside the silence in the car. Margaret parked in the space farthest from the stores and turned off the ignition and said, "I think I'd like to meet Stephanie."

An impossibility of course, but for a second he imagined them sitting in Stephanie's kitchen. What would they have said about him? She grabbed the invitations, and he walked after her, caught up with her, passed her, and opened the door. A clerk was waiting behind a counter.

"These are the wrong color," Margaret said and held up the offending box. Jonathan moved up beside her.

The clerk couldn't have been more than eighteen. Maybe she was twenty. She was slumped against the counter, staring down at a paperback. "Do you have your receipt?" she asked, just on the edge of antagonistic, and suddenly they had found a common enemy.

"I have it here," Jonathan said. He fished around in his pocket.

"They usually put them in the box," the girl said. "Right on top."

"Then *of course* we have it," Margaret said, and she dropped the box onto the counter.

The girl took off the lid. "It's not here," she said.

"It was in there," Jonathan said. "You must recognize me. I was in here yesterday." *He* didn't recognize *her*. There had been more people in the store then. He had run in and run out.

"No," she said, not looking at him.

"Fuck this," he said, and he took a step to the door, then a step back to get the box. As he picked it up he said, "Where's your manager, anyway?" But it wasn't really a question. He was halfway gone.

"We'll just cancel the credit card, you know," Margaret said as a parting shot, a lesson in practicality. It was amazing how angry they were now. It was almost beautiful.

"I'll come back tomorrow when someone else is working," he said as they were walking across the parking lot, and suddenly it seemed as if they had won an important battle quickly and decisively.

He said, "She was a real idiot. Can you believe that?" He was driving now. Somehow he had ended up with the keys.

"Let's just forget about it," she said. "We'll get them reprinted. Somewhere else. We have plenty of time still."

"She really got to me," he said.

Margaret said, "Me too."

"I can't stand people like that."

They stopped for food, and as they waited for more coffee, they looked at each other over the greasy table. He put some bills and change down and heard it clatter against the Formica. It was the money he had in his pocket after paying the taxi driver last night. He put his keys on the table and then a ticket stub from a movie. He emptied his pockets. He said, "I was thinking of a new project. I think this other one has reached a dead end. I think it's getting to me, you know? I think it's really getting to me."

At other tables people were smacking ketchup onto their eggs and wiping the faces of their babies. The action in each booth seemed self-contained, like the activity in the cars on the road outside, and urgent somehow. The hands reaching across tables. The retelling of movies and television shows. The elderly couple eating without speaking, heads bowed slightly. Jonathan passed Margaret the sugar. She tore the top off a half-and-half container and dribbled it into her coffee.

She said, "I think that's a good idea."

The possibility of losing her now seemed as matter-of-fact as everything else in the restaurant. It had been real before too, but he hadn't seen it until she was sitting squarely across from him, and he was looking into her eyes. The waitress asked if they were ready, and he told her no, could they have another minute? Music was playing from the kitchen. He could see the cook through a small window.

"Look," he said, "I'm sorry. I don't know what's been happening with me. I don't know why I did that. It's like I was dredging all this stuff up."

"Past tense," she said.

"Past tense," he repeated, and he put his finger on a dime and slid it to the edge of the table. The waitress came over again, and they picked something to order out of the air—more food than they needed and more coffee, and they thanked her with genuine smiles. The waitress had a heavy, motherly body, close-cropped hair, a patient voice.

He wondered if Margaret was as surprised as he was to smile so sincerely at her. She smiled back, and when she had gone on to the next table, Jonathan said, "I'm sorry. I'm sorry. I'm sorry."

She handed him a napkin. He was crying. He took it from her and pushed it around his face. The food would be coming soon.

"Christ," he said. People were watching. They were looking at their food, but they were looking at him too. They were sneaking a peek between bites, between sentences, and then only later, in the car on the way home, would they turn to their partner and say, "What was up with that guy?"

But this was necessary. A public display. It was a kind of penance. A baby was crying too, from somewhere behind him. It moaned with a pain that seemed impossible, a howl that bordered on rage. The sound of it made more tears come. He touched his face, his nose, his eyes and thought of the words his father said that day in the basement as they looked at the photographs.

"I'm sorry," he said again, this time for his strange loss of control, and then another sorry for apologizing so much, and the baby wasn't making noise anymore, but he was—a low, wet bleat. And yet he wondered how much of this was real. He felt as if he had tapped into that deep place certain actors occupy when performing an especially difficult scene.

He cupped his face in his hands, closed his eyes, and lowered his head, slumping forward until he was resting on the table. If what Stephanie had said were true—if she *had* looked frightened in that one photograph—then what had frightened her? The possibility that it might be *him* seemed completely ridiculous, especially today as he sat in front of his fiancée bawling like a child. But when Margaret's fingers touched the top of his head and began tentatively stroking his hair, he almost jumped up and warned her away.

That afternoon they sent the invitations out into the world. They were good enough.

Candy was lost and I hoped I might find him somewhere in the graffiti-scribbled buildings of our youth. Or it was *me* who was lost. So I left my wife and daughter and drove north through six states back to that ruined Victorian house on the hill where Cheryl was throwing her never ending party.

I entered through the wide-open back door, walked into the smoke filled pantry, found a beer, and held it like I belonged. People wandered from room to room, sat on the floors, passed around black bottles of wine, pills wrapped in strips of cellophane. Most were strangers—fragile little potheads dressed in secondhand clothes, Hispanic kids from the westside projects, and even a couple of beefy jocks in letter jackets checking out the freak show. They were probably strangers to Cheryl too, people she had met a couple of days before in a coffeehouse or club. They glanced at me as I moved deeper into the house. A few older ones pulled me close and said my name—the name they used to call me. I hadn't heard it in years.

Her letter had said that everything was okay. But it didn't feel okay. The walls in the front room were spray-painted with sunflowers and smiley faces, and the floors were littered with plastic cups, bent cans, scraps of paper, ghostly strands of toilet tissue I broke with my legs as I crossed the room to Cheryl. A band was grinding slow familiar chords in another room. I set down the beer on a windowsill, took her by the arm, and pulled her to a corner, where a couple of skeleton-faced boys were sneaking *manteca*. As she kissed my cheek I said, "He's not here?"

"We don't know where he is," she said and something else that was drowned out by the band's building intensity. A girl was jumping on a caved-in couch, arms tight by her sides and teeth locked in a speed grimace. A few people sprawled on the floor looking up at her, and as the music swelled she turned in a circle, corkscrewing, and they applauded and hooted. Cheryl raised her voice to compete with the music, but there was something creeping and languid in her tone. I wondered what she had taken.

She had buzz-cut her hair and dyed the leftovers bright red, and she looked better than I thought she might, like some of the sophisticated forty-something women who came to my readings and asked me sensitive questions about my history. She put her hand on my back and pulled me closer, my fingers still wrapped around her arm, and for a second I thought we might kiss. "I didn't think you'd make it," she said.

"You knew I would," I said, although I wasn't sure she could hear me over the music. A kid with a yellow scarf wrapped around his shaved skull came over to her, whispered something in her ear, and she pushed a couple of twenties into his palm—maybe for drugs, maybe just charity.

She said something as she looked out over the crowd, and I bent my head closer to listen. She repeated what she had said, evenly and clearly, like it was a line she was practicing for a play. "If you hadn't run away you wouldn't have had to come back." I straightened up and loosened my grip. "Do you at least miss him?" she added clear as a bell.

I realized the music had paused, and I squeezed a few words into the pocket of silence between songs. "It's not like he died," I said, but maybe he was dead and this was what passed for his wake.

Then I heard it. Someone was singing one of his old songs from the back of the house, probably because they had spotted me. I knew the words—sarcastic and nasty when skittering over a backward Black Sabbath riff, beautiful when sung with an acoustic guitar. I could tell Cheryl remembered it too, because she tilted up her chin and closed her eyes. Someone else joined in, harmonizing badly. *It's the most beautiful river running through the most beautiful town in the most beautiful world in the world. The most beautiful world in the world.*

The party moved around us, past us, and now my mind reeled back fifteen years and three city blocks to the warehouse on Canal Street, where we used to watch Candy smack around a guitar with his revolving-door band. I remembered the coiled energy of his body, the flailing of his right hand, and the nervousness of the little crowd of dropouts, wannabe ecoterrorists, dopers, and ex-lovers as they gathered around him in a loose half-circle. They wanted to see him scratch his fingers along the strings like he was clawing an itch, jerking out chords in spasms and squinting his eyes as if against glaring light.

I wondered if they were waiting for him to step through the door of Cheryl's house right then, the way I had five minutes earlier. We would pull each other close, the room would go quiet, and then with some urging Candy would take a guitar from the band and play one of the old songs. Everything would be fine then, right?

As if I had said these thoughts aloud, Cheryl laughed and slipped my grip, spinning back out to the center of the room and then toward the kitchen. I followed her, stepping over a couple of people staring at the ceiling. "Hello," one of them said as I looked down, and we shared vague smiles.

Cheryl headed outside to the cracked blacktop driveway on the side of the house. People were drinking out there and throwing a soccer ball at the broken basketball hoop. I could see her through the kitchen window, talking to a teenage girl who had come probably because she heard the noise. They were laughing, and Cheryl looked much older then, around the eyes especially. I probably looked older too.

"Hey, hey," someone said from behind me, and I knew the voice. I knew the face too, although he had gained weight and grown a beard to match his stringy hair. I had forgotten the name, but he used to play bass in Candy's band.

"I heard you singing that song," I said. "It's been years since I heard that."

He lifted his head and wiped his nose with his thumb and finger. "I have your book. I haven't cracked it yet. Things have been crazy obviously. Things have been out of control, man."

I tried to get away from him, but he motormouthed after me, through the kitchen and past a circle of people handing around the nub of a joint. He stopped long enough to close his eyes and take a deep drag and then said in a louder voice, "Who would have thought things would turn out the way they did?"

"Nobody," I said. "Not me anyway. Especially not me."

He laughed through his nose, blowing smoke, and held the joint out to me. "His father still lives here, you know. We drove by his place the other day and thought about going in and asking him where the hell was Candy. You know, really lay some interrogation on him. We thought about throwing rocks at the windows too."

My own father was in a veterans' hospital in Providence with a tumor in the front of his brain. I went to see him whenever I drove through Rhode Island, which was not often. He sometimes called me by my brother's name, and I let him, because it seemed to give him some solace, and my brother was even less inclined to visit him than I was. Besides, it was more comfortable to visit him as someone else, like wearing a disguise. The last time I went I sat at the foot of his bed, and we watched television, and he complained about the food and the nurses and said that the other inmates—he called the patients inmates—were trying to steal from him. He had a Semper Fi tattoo on his inner forearm, but it had collapsed into nonsense as he lost weight. His weak hands shook when he held a spoon. Once or twice I tried to talk to him about our past, but I always pulled up short. What did I want anyway? To make this chapped-lipped old man feel guilty? Yes, probably. But the fog in his mind made him safe. It was like a shield my words couldn't penetrate. Then again, maybe it was just an act—his disguise.

"Dad," I said, "do you remember what you used to do to me?" I was testing him, poking around the edges of his memory.

"I used to take you kids fishing at Round Pond," he mumbled. "You and your friends. We would get up so early in the morning."

These were the kind of stories he told now. His cancer sto-

CRYBABY 119

ries—that's how I thought of them. And none of them were true. Maybe they were wishes rising from his dank subconscious, pushed free by the pressure of the knot in his skull. I guess I didn't care too much, except that I had to listen to them and consider, at least for a second, that they might be real.

"The roads were so empty, going to that pond," he said. "It was like we were the only people alive out there."

On the television the Red Sox were behind by a couple of runs. The other team had men on first and third but Pedro Martinez was pitching, and he looked as angry as I had ever seen him. He threw one strike, then another, and looked up at the sky—talking to God, I guess—but Dad just called him an asshole and jabbed the remote duct-taped to the bed rail. In the following silence I rubbed his feet and felt the fragile bones of his toes between my thumb and forefinger. His eyes closed and he slept, looking peaceful—like the kind of father who really would have done the things he had just talked about.

"Okay," I said to the man who had sung Candy's song. "What the hell? For old time's sake," and I took the little wet roach between my fingers.

I had been Candy's best friend since middle school, when he was still breaking windows and setting small fires. He had learned to play some primitive songs and then to write them, and by high school small crowds took the freight elevator up nine stories to see him practice with his band.

I remember those days as a haze of noise and motion. The onlookers loved it when his bowling shirt opened and they could see the scar, jagged on his stomach like an old road running across a map. His right arm would pump, his hand shimmering across the strings, and the shirt would open and close and blow like a flag behind him. The windows were always up even if it was cold outside, and the yellow walls would sweat in summertime, and I swear you could smell the fish in the river a hundred feet below.

Candy didn't care, not about the smell or the heat, not about the audience, and not even about the other people in his band, who always seemed to be falling behind. Sometimes he grabbed a smoke and let them catch up or jam on their own, the guitar hanging loose at his waist as he slid a cigarette between his lips. Or he glanced out one of the tall warehouse windows at the traffic speeding below, and then he spun on the ball of his foot and attacked the microphone, barked at it like he was going to chew it up and spit it out.

My favorite song was "Crybaby," and the first time he played it in his bedroom sitting on the edge of his narrow cot the world stopped. "Crybaby," he sang softly, "can't you take a little scrape? Can't you take a little bruise?" He wore a black knit cap on his shaved head, head bowed, and his right eye was freshly blackened, his nose red and swollen. "Turn that frown upside down, Crybaby, Crybaby, Crybaby." The space between syllables opened up and closed, lengthened and shortened each time he sang the word. His hand hung above the same shaky G and then came down, and it rang out like the only G chord ever struck. I don't know how he did it. Maybe it was just me.

"Crybaby, Crybaby, Crybaby." The chords clattered louder, and his voice rose and cracked and bounced around the walls, and it seemed like the song could go on forever. Would go on forever. It was our song, *my* song. I knew what that blackened eye felt like, had worn two myself in the last year.

Later when Candy sang it in public his eyes always found mine in the crowd, if only for a second, and he smiled as he launched into the chorus, and I bet every girl between us thought he was looking at her and only her. Later still the chorus vanished altogether—Candy probably figured the crowd knew that part by heart anyway—and the song grew even more jagged and out of control. That was when he was taking a lot of amphetamines. His newest drummer had a lifeline to unlimited sources in New York, and the stuff just appeared in our pockets.

That's how Candy got his nickname. He would cup his hand to his mouth and swallow and say, "Sweet." We were just kids. Not even twenty then.

"When's the last time you saw him?" I asked as I passed back the joint to the guy who had attached himself to me. "Was he okay?"

"I bet they'll turn it into a movie," he said. "Do you think they'll turn it into a movie?" He was twirling this idea around in his head now, absorbed in the possibilities. "Who would play you?" he asked. "Who would play Candy? They'd probably get people who look nothing like you. Who's enough of an asshole to play your dad? Or Candy's dad. They should get one guy to play both parts. With a mustache and without."

He laughed like that was the funniest thing he had ever heard.

"It's just a stupid book," I said. But what I wanted to say was, "It's just my life." My life it seemed then, with the people who had once occupied it swirling around me, should not have been turned into that book, let alone a movie. It wouldn't have been either if a small press in upstate New York hadn't recognized "something there" in my draft and then been patient enough to bring it through three rounds of edits. They said the subject matter was genuine, the people were real, and I had a distinct journalistic voice. They said it was a story that deserved—that needed—to be told.

"This book of yours, is it popular?" the guy asked, which was a way of asking if I was rich, if he might see me on TV soon.

"No," I said. "It's only been reviewed a couple of places and not very well."

"Oh yeah?"

"Yeah," I said, remembering the day I had spread the paper at the kitchen table and read the first review. "One guy used the words melodramatic and unrealistic. I don't think he believed people like us really exist. And in such abundance." I waved my hand across the undulating crowd, the bobbing heads and shaking bodies.

"Don't worry about it. You'll bounce back. You're a survivor," he said. Which meant, I think, that Candy was not.

"What?" I said with a sneer in my voice.

"The reviews around here aren't so hot either," he added as he looked around for something else to put in his mouth. "Like I said, I haven't read it. I've really never been much of a reader. But from what I hear on the street, you left out the best parts."

He was still smiling but he took a step back. I took a step forward. He wasn't expecting that kind of challenge—especially from me—and he said something under his breath. My nickname. I thought of the source of that name—my father—and those visits to his narrow hospital room. He had not called me that name in a long time, but I knew it was hidden somewhere down deep in his brain, a little smudge of anger and disgust.

"Only my friends call me that," I said, "and not even them anymore."

He began to sing the song again, his voice sweet and mocking. I glanced to my right at a laughing girl. She was holding plastic cups to her eyes like binoculars and looking at the ceiling, looking through the ceiling for all I knew. She was laughing with her mouth open. But the laugh turned into a yell as she turned her head toward us, and the cups dropped from her hands and people were holding me, pulling me backward out of the room. I was dimly aware that I had just thrown a punch, striking the man on the chin and knocking him off his feet. I threw a second halfhearted one at the empty air, and I thought even as they were dragging me away, *what a stupid thing to do. How fake.*

Two teenagers held me loosely by the arms. One of them said, "Peace, amigo, peace," and the other said, "Chill, okay? Just calm down," and I let myself go limp there on the porch. Candy and I had talked about quick acts of violence that might free us, savoring the punches and kicks we'd land, the traps we'd set, the places we'd escape to afterward.

I remember him saying, "They're the same son of a bitch anyway," once when we were standing on a bridge watching the traffic slide below us, and then he made the sound of a car horn, a bleating, painful, comical sound that made a real car beep back. One hand was cupped to his mouth and the other was holding the wire fence, and it seemed that if he had jumped at that moment he would have flown. I would fight his demons. He would fight mine.

This punch had not felt like anything Candy and I imagined. Which is not to say it felt bad. "El loco," one of the teenagers said, and he pushed my shoulder. They looked like brothers—the same pug nose, the same small eyes and jet-black hair—sixteen or so, both of them, about half my age. "Drink this," one of them said. "It'll make you feel better." And he handed me some flat orange soda in a plastic cup. I swallowed it down, dropped the cup, breathed deep.

My knuckle was bleeding just above my wedding ring, and I remembered that my wife had asked me to call her as soon as I arrived. But the idea of talking to her on the phone seemed impossible now—or at least beyond my ability.

I sucked my knuckle and wondered how hard that first punch had connected. The two brothers were laughing, and I had to laugh too—a snort that made them grin and slap my shoulder. Maybe they knew who I was, and maybe they didn't, but they seemed to be treating me with respect. I was a man who had just thrown a dirty punch. That could have been enough to do it. Maybe they hated the guy I hit.

We were cackling like we had just heard the filthiest, funniest joke in Lawrence, Massachusetts. But I was laughing at a different joke, a private one only Candy and I would understand. I was thinking of the little electrical thrill when my fist connected, the way the guy's expression flashed from a self-satisfied grin to childish shock as he stumbled back. Would he wake up the next day with a bruise? Two hundred something pages, two years of my life, a mess of theories and guesswork about motivations and feelings, and it was one lame-ass punch that helped me get into my father's head.

The old house on Primrose had burned down, like the house next to it had years ago, and the vinyl siding of the buildings on either side was blistered and blackened. Enough empty space was there now for a McDonald's or a Burger King. In six months I would probably be able to return and find one. I stood on the side of the road drinking bottled water and listening to the cars pass behind my back as they headed to the highway. This was where Candy and a few of the others had lived and where they had thrown parties like the one I just came from.

It wasn't surprising to me that the house was gone. The landlord owned a number of buildings in town, and several of them had burned down. And this one had almost been destroyed when the house next door had burned. I had told the story in the book, beginning with my waking up on the couch in the middle of the night, the room flickering orange. People were yelling outside, but I was still half asleep, and drunk, and so I sat there watching the flames through the window like it was television. Candy appeared, naked except for a towel, and Cheryl too, and we all watched from the window until the firemen pounded at the door.

"It's magic," Cheryl said, and then the door opened, and Candy went to get his blue jeans and his guitar.

Outside a few people were crying, but for the most part the neighborhood had the atmosphere of a block party, and I remember shoeless and shirtless Candy sitting on the curb and playing songs. Some of the neighbors gathered around to listen, kids feigning disinterest, middle-aged wives checking him out.

Someone passed around cigarettes and cans of Coke and little hard sweets wrapped in yellow foil, and Candy told jokes to the smallest kids, jokes I had never heard before. He played songs I didn't know he knew. "Strawberry Fields Forever," the verses in Spanish for the old ladies. *Es fácil vivir con ojos cerrados, mal entendiendo todo lo que ves, se hace difícil ser alguien, pero eso está bien, no me importa demasiado.* Then he did "Danny Boy," his voice high and keening, like he was making fun of not just our sadness but of sadness as a concept. A few people joined in, including Cheryl, who was drinking a beer and dancing a high-stepping Greek dance.

When this other fire had hit—the fire that leveled his place and sent him off in some mysterious direction—Candy had probably been alone. I guessed that he had not played his guitar on the curb and that maybe he had not played it for a long time. I didn't know if he even owned a guitar anymore.

In the letter Cheryl said she had gone by there the next morning, after she had found out. I'm sure she half expected him to be sleeping behind the convenience store, but he was nowhere to be found. He hadn't been talking to anyone recently, and she wondered if he had moved before the fire had hit. She went home, made a few phone calls, and then she thought of me. She had heard about the book, and I was his brother in spirit, after all. At least that's how she put it in the letter. I folded it and put it away and after three days I had almost forgotten it, but then I got the call from the hospital. They said my father was asking for me, that he was nervous and anxious. After playing the role of the dutiful son—asking the right questions, then telling them I would be there soon—I hung up the phone, took the letter out of a drawer, smoothed it out, and read it again. I left the next day, and here I was, watching the vacant lot where Candy once lived, like something might actually happen if I just stared long enough.

I finished my water and capped it and crossed the street, where I called my wife from the greasy pay phone. A group of kids watched me from their car as if I were up to no good. They revved the engine and clicked their headlights from low to high at their friend as she came out of the store, paper bag in hand. She climbed in, the engine revved again, they backed out into the street, and I was alone.

"Hello?" she said.

"Melissa," I said.

I could tell I had awakened her. She hesitated, and I could hear her breathing before she said, "I thought you'd call sooner. How is everything going up there?"

"It could be worse," I said. "I'm calling from a pay phone. I don't have a lot of minutes on my phone card so we should be quick."

"Right," she said. "Okay. Quick. What are you going to do?"

"I don't know. Maybe I'll head back tonight. It's been a disappointing trip so far. I'm not sure what I was trying to accomplish."

"I'm not sure either," she said. "They called again from the hospital. It's worse."

"I figured," I said, and then, not wanting to head further in that direction, "How's Kayla?"

The phone clicked and I thought we had been disconnected, but then her voice came back to me. "She's fine. She's been asleep for hours. She was waiting for your phone call too, you know."

A car pulled next to the phone and beeped its horn once—a shrill, sustained blast—and then a kid in a baseball cap and oversized leather jacket jumped out of the passenger door. "What?" I asked. "Sorry. I can't hear you. It's noisy here."

"I asked you what you're going to do now. If you're going to get a hotel."

"I'm going to see the old man."

"Good."

"Not my father. Candy's dad. He still lives here." There was another beep of the horn, another silence between us. "Melissa?" I said.

She said, "You sound strange."

"I know. But I'm okay. It's like riding a bicycle, coming back here."

"That's not what I mean," she said.

"I know what you mean," I said. "And don't worry. I love you very much."

"You said it was like riding a bicycle."

"The roads. I was just talking about the roads. Finding my way around."

She seemed to consider this as she took another long breath. Then she said, "I love you too. Like crazy, you know?"

I pictured her sitting up in bed, the phone cord twirled around her wrist, eyes closed as she imagined me at this phone booth, shoulders slumped, holding the phone in two hands. "The same," I said. "The same."

"Then don't worry me."

"Okay. Then I won't worry you. It just all seems so immediate now that I'm back here. It all seems *important*. Like I never left. Well, not really. It's like I left last week and changed my mind." But that wasn't right either. I didn't know what I meant, and I wondered if I would ever be capable of eyeing the truth and hitting it dead center. At that moment Candy seemed to be the kind of person who could do that, and if he was, it somehow meant I was not. "I'm not feeling very well," I said.

"I can tell," she said. "I do trust you. But I feel like I know those people. And I think they're dangerous."

"Just because of some words I wrote down," I said, and I was surprised by the edge in my voice. "That's why you know them."

"Yes," she said. "Because of some words. *Your* words."

"Well, then you don't know them at all," I said. "I'm not sure what I'm trying to tell you."

"I'm not sure either. What are you trying to tell me?"

I took a deep breath. "Just that I need to visit Candy's dad, that I'll be home as soon as possible, and that I love you very much." I hung up the phone and wiped my hand on my pants. The world was splintering into pieces of color, and I wondered what had been in that orange drink I swallowed at the party. The car was beeping again, and I imagined Melissa sitting in the dark bedroom still holding the phone.

We had been married for two years when I began work on the book. Although she supported me, she was perplexed that a person with such an unremarkable past would want to write it all down for . . . who? My father had just been hospitalized, and we still lived close enough that I visited him often. I sat at the foot of his bed and listened to him talk. As the visits continued I realized I couldn't reply the way I wanted to except in private, using a pen and paper and then, after I had filled an entire notebook with scribbles, a typewriter.

"So you didn't get along," Melissa had said once as I worked at the kitchen table after Kayla was in bed. "Lots of sons don't get along with their fathers." I had not told her much except to say that there was friction between us. The details came to her through the book, which she read chapter by chapter, correcting misspellings and grammar with a red pen. That's how she got to know Candy and the rest of them. I wondered if she saw them less as real people, more as my personal literary creations. I was seeing them that way too — as characters I had placed on a stage and given words to speak. It took Cheryl's letter to remind me how real Candy was, how unreal I might be without him. When I had told Melissa, "Candy's in trouble," she had said, "Oh, the boy from the book."

As I stepped away from the phone, I took one last look at the space where the houses had been. All that absence seemed like a fitting monument.

I had figured at least one small thing out. So I had to make a third stop that night.

I could see the blue glow of the television from the back porch. And on the other side of the room a figure sat in a chair, hunched over an aluminum tray. The TV cast light across his body, but I couldn't see his face. It had to be him though, and I knocked on the door. Tapped actually, on the small inset window where a sign had been affixed with masking tape. *Beware of Dog.* He had never owned a dog but had put the sign up to keep people away, and after a while we started calling *him* the dog as much as the old man. Sometimes we called him *bestia* or Frankenstein or even Papa Smurf when we felt charitable. We had endless nicknames for him, although usually we kept him at arm's length with a pronoun, as in *You wouldn't believe what he just did,* or *Someday he'll get what's coming to him.* The window was stained glass, little red and white fractals forming an angel — too nice for a place like this. It had always looked more like a bird with a bowed head and spread wings. I had considered breaking it once, but thinking about it was as far as I could go.

"Come in," someone called over the TV, and I opened the door.

Every house has its own smell, like a fingerprint, deep and complicated as a story. I remembered the smell of this house — cigarettes, of course, and the thin, bony fish his dad always cooked, and the cheap air freshener he used to try to cover it all up. Someone was laughing on the TV.

I crossed the room and touched the small kitchen table with

things strewn across it. Two newspapers, one rolled up in a rubber band, the other open to the sports page. A coffee cup. A piece of paper with a few words scrawled across it. Needlenose pliers. Some coins. A seashell with the tip broken off. I lifted the shell and knew that Candy was there. It was as large as my palm, and I cupped it to my ear, hearing the same ocean Candy had probably heard when he picked it up off Hampton Beach. We always used to go there in the winter, walking up and down the surf with our cold hands stuffed in our pockets.

"Crybaby," someone said. The same voice—snide, nasal. I wanted to hug him. I wanted to pull his mouth to my ear like the opening of the shell and hear that voice tell me everything that had happened in the years we had been apart.

"People are worried," I said.

"Boo hoo," he said and curled his lips the way he used to when he played the guitar. He was balding so that his hairline formed a blunt black arrow down his scalp, and he had gained a lot of weight around his midriff, although his face was narrow and his cheeks sunken. Too much beer and speed maybe. The eyes were the same—small and dark like obsidian—but if I had passed him on the street I'm not sure I would have recognized him.

He was wearing a gray T-shirt and jeans, and around his neck hung a beaded necklace. A gift from Cheryl probably, something that had survived the fire because he had been wearing it. "I'm doing an Elvis," he explained before I could ask the question, and then, "I'm helping out with my dad," like the fire hadn't happened. "He's turned into a puppy dog, if you can believe it. It's ridiculous."

"You probably shouldn't call me that," I said.

"Yeah," he said. "I've read the book. I've read it twice. I bet you didn't think I knew about it, but word trickles down—even to here. "He picked up the coffee cup from the kitchen table and put it in the sink, ran water into it.

"I didn't lie though," I said.

"You want something from me," he said. "I can tell."

"Yeah," I said. "I want to know you're all right."

"I liked the stuff about your mom especially," he said. "It was beautiful. It really was. I remember those grilled cheese sandwiches too. You got that all down."

"Thank you," I said. "That means a lot to me."

"But I'm not so sure about what you wrote about me, Crybaby. I was never that pretty. I was never that talented." He snickered and lowered his voice to a theatrical whisper. "It's like you wrote the book to seduce me all over again."

"Can I sit down?" I asked. The kitchen felt small and hot like something was cooking in the oven. I rested my hand on the back of a chair.

"And I thought you and I, we shared everything," he continued, "but a couple of things in there—things your dad did—they were a surprise to me. The cigarette burns. Did you keep that secret from me, or did you make it up?" He lifted the change, rattled it around in his hand like dice he was about to throw, and put it in his pocket. His voice sounded like two voices—one mocking, one loving—and then the two voices split into four and then into eight. It felt like I was talking to a crowd, and I wanted to fall asleep right there on his father's kitchen floor. I sat down instead and put my arm on the table, still holding the shell. The ceiling flew around my head, and the shell turned in my hand like a gear. I could feel it moving slowly, and I decided that it was somehow connected to the ceiling above me and to Candy's mouth and the television in the next room. It was some kind of remote control, but I didn't know how to work it.

"It was inspiring, though," Candy was saying. "I identified with the protagonist." He laughed, and the TV laughed, and I swore I heard his father say, "Shut up in there." So I muttered something about having to leave, that my wife was probably worried about me, that I wasn't feeling well. But I was far below Candy now, as if he was standing on a box looking down at me. I realized my knee had touched the floor.

"You look awful," he said, and he touched my hair.

"I know. And you don't look so good either."

We laughed then the way we used to, and I remembered him once saying, with a fresh triangular bruise on his cheek, "You know what makes him angry? When you look him right in the face and snicker. If you giggle he hates that." We had always compared notes.

Candy had his hands on my shoulders and he was rubbing, working the muscles. His hand slid down to the point high on my chest where my collarbone had been broken. He slid two fingers over the bone nub, the way he used to, and then down deeper into my shirt. "You'll be okay in a couple of hours," he said.

"I know," I said, and I tried to turn around on my knees, little baby steps in a circle, until I was looking at his thighs and distended belly. I hugged him lightly, and he took me by the shoulders and tried to help me stand.

"The problem with memoirs is that they're written by the successful," Candy said. "They're written by the people who get out." One hand rose from my shoulder and touched my cheek. "We're not the same."

"I'm sorry," I said. Or at least thought. I tried to focus on his words instead of on the blaring television. The sound came from above us and underneath us, and I hoped that I wasn't going to be sick. I took a deep breath and smelled his father's breakfast—greasy specks of burned egg and butter and coffee—and remembered something from the book. The thought descended on me like a spider on a web. What had I written? That Candy's pain was a way to measure my own.

"I missed you," I said, or thought I said, and pushed my face forward into the folds of Candy's pants. I tried to move my lips, and his hand steered my head. He made a low humming as I nuzzled him thinking, *he is almost singing*. It sounded like something from the book, as if this would find a place there too, next to our childhoods, like boxes on a shelf.

"I really missed you," I said, and this time I knew I had spoken aloud, because he said the same thing back to me, and then he told me to stop.

I could hear voices from the other room, spoons scraping in bowls, footsteps across the floor. I opened my eyes to darkness, but some light shone through the cracks in the window blinds, and I could see stacks of books piled high on either side of the mattress, red and yellow candles stuck in empty wine bottles, and small piles of sweaters and flower-print dresses. Cheryl's room.

She sat at the foot of the bed, rubbing my thigh through the quilt. I allowed myself to think of my father in his hospital room—to make that awkward poetic connection and then dispense with it. My shoulder hurt. I could still feel Candy on my lips. "Hey, sleeping beauty," she said. "Want some water?"

"Sure," I said, and she handed me the glass she had been drinking from. My throat was dry and my voice sounded deep and weary, but I felt better than I had thought I might. My leg was shaking a little, vibrating almost, which was probably why

Cheryl was rubbing it. Her face was marked with red splotches, her mascara was streaked, and I noticed some thin mysterious cuts on her neck, crusted with dried blood. I wondered if something bad had happened the night before, a drama worse than the one I had created with my stupid punch—or maybe connected to it.

"They're eating grapefruit in the other room," she said as I handed her back the empty glass. "It's always good to have fruit and water the next day."

She told me this as if I were new here, but I remembered the ritual—Cheryl cutting the grapefruits in half with a long knife, passing them around, sharing stories from the night before and laughing at our stupidity. I wondered if she still picked up data entry projects whenever she needed money, if she begged her parents for cash when times were tight, who she was sleeping with and if they caused her a lot of pain and heartache. I suppose Candy and I had.

"Thank you," I said. "I could use some. I had a bad night."

"You make your own trouble," she said, and I was surprised by the flatness in her voice. I wasn't sure if she was talking about me or people in general.

I pushed back the quilt and sat up. I was still dressed and my clothes were damp with sweat. "I found him," I said, because I thought that might balance the damage I had caused. This was, after all, why she had written to me, why I had come back here.

"I thought you might," she said. "See how easy it was?"

"He looked bad," I said, as I climbed off the mattress and eyed the cluttered floor for my shoes.

"It's funny how people stay the same," she said, and I immediately resented her for stealing my private thoughts and sharing them with me like they were hers. "When I first saw you last night you were just standing there not talking to anybody, and you had this look on your face, almost serene, and that's when it occurred to me that you are a dad now. I thought, *maybe he's changed.* But of course you haven't."

I bent down and found my left shoe, still laced tightly, and the ball of my sock pushed down inside it. She had taken care of me pretty well when I had returned to her house, telling me I was in no condition to drive and then taking me upstairs to her room, past people talking on the stairs in hushed tones. The party had grown smaller, more serious, and the stragglers seemed like different people—gentle and sincere.

"I don't know what you're talking about," I said to her, as I stretched out my sock and slipped it over my foot, scanning the room for the other half of the pair. The second shoe was going to be more difficult to find.

"That's just like you," she said. "You were always putting yourself in jeopardy and blaming it on other people."

"I did not," I said. "I do not."

"Boo hoo hoo," she said, almost exactly like Candy had done. "His father was worse than yours. Much worse. Everybody here knows that." I didn't say anything, so she added, "And you *had* a mother, at least while you were growing up. Candy just had me." She shrugged and spread her arms slightly, as if to show off this poor substitute.

I found the second shoe behind a fallen stack of books. I must have kicked them over during the night. I began to restack them—old mystery paperbacks and water-damaged philosophy textbooks and thin collections of poetry. "Please do not go through my stuff," she said. "Just leave it, okay?"

"Okay," I said. "Sure."

"I do have it, if that's what you're searching for."

"I'm not searching for anything," I said.

"Sure you are," she said. "You're always searching for your-self. That's what you do."

I stood on one leg and tried to put on my sock as fast as I could, bouncing to keep my balance. She stepped toward me, and I thought she might push me over, but she started going through the books, lifting them and tossing them aside. "It's in here somewhere," she said. A wine bottle tipped and began to roll across the floor, but she caught it and righted it.

Any second she would find it and read my words back to me. I imagined her speaking them in an elevated, pretentious parody of my voice, moving through the scenes, pointing out the gaps, the hidden places. She would find the scene about that first fire, with Candy naked except for the towel, his body glowing orange, and say, "This is wrong. You were in the same bed that night. Why didn't you write that?" She would find another place like that, and then another, and I would bend my head, working the laces of my shoes, and listen.

"Look at this," she said, and she laughed at her discovery, although I could not see what she had in her hands.

"Where are my keys?" I said.

I left that place, traveled the eight hours in six, ready to tell everything. I parked the car, took the front stairs two at a time, opened the unlocked door. Stepping through the darkened house I found Melissa in the bedroom, hands raised to her ear as she gazed out a window. She was taking out her earrings. I crossed the room and wrapped my arms around her.

"He's gone," she said.

SWIMMING IN THE DARK

When I was young my mother sometimes woke in the middle of the night, the way people do in small houses where noise doesn't have far to travel. She would pull her bathrobe tight around her, walk downstairs, and find my brother at the kitchen table hunched over a book. I don't think they talked much, although she might have put some water on to boil, or turned the thermostat up, or poured him a glass of orange juice. Then she'd sit down with her cup of coffee and watch him read.

"Alex was always working hard," she told me once, "on something or other."

After Alex was gone his sleeplessness moved into me and grew skittish and aimless, so that by the time I reached my early teens I spent most nights wandering the house. At these times I wanted nothing more than to fall quickly and completely into sleep, to rest my head on my pillow and let my thinking wind itself down to nothing. But it was also at these times, and only at these times, that I seemed granted the ability to recognize things for what they truly were. The noise and false light of the day would recede, and I would notice the shape of a lamp, or the cold grit of the kitchen floor, or the sound of the oil burner clicking in the cellar.

It was on one of these restless nights that I found my mother on the back porch looking out at our small square yard. Sometimes we sat out there on Sunday mornings listening to the bells of the Catholic church ringing across town, but this wasn't morning, and although I wanted to, I did not go outside and sit down beside her. I stood looking through the broken screen door, trying to see whatever she saw off in the gray shadows of our property.

She must have heard me or felt my eyes on her, because she turned and smiled and said, "Hello, Tom," as if it were perfectly natural for us to be where we were at that hour. "I just decided to get some fresh air," she said and she held up her cigarette for me to see. "I know what you're thinking, Tom," she said. "You're thinking this is going to be the same." She patted the step next to her in invitation. "You're a smart boy," she said, although I knew that wasn't really true.

I opened the door and stepped out. When I sat next to her she put her hand on mine and squeezed as if to calm me. I could see her fingers in the light from the porch lamp. Dried blood collected on one side of her thumb where the cuticle had been bitten red. When she noticed me looking she clasped both hands in her lap. "I've been trying to quit again," she said, and I nodded in sympathy. Many times I had seen my mother crumple her cigarette pack and calculate with pen and paper how much money she would save in a week, a month, a year.

She said, "There was a time I figured I would go on this

way for the rest of my life. But not anymore. I don't want a big change. I just want to see what might happen." Her hand moved to my knee for a moment. "You know, Tom," she said, "these are difficult times. We all have to be flexible. Sue has to be flexible. You're the youngest and I know it's hard for you, but you have to be flexible too." She smiled as if she had told a joke. "I'm trying to be flexible, God knows. And Harris, well, he's trying really hard too."

"He seems nice," I said. I imagined Harris asleep in my mother's bed, head deep in the pillow, the way I had seen him the first time he slept over, several weekends before. He'd slept in her bed every Friday and Saturday night since then.

"He *is* nice. I've talked to him about you. I've talked to him about Sue. He gave me some good advice. He said this was a difficult time for you. He's the one who mentioned being flexible actually."

"Well, that's good," I said.

"He knows a lot about children. You might not think that, but he does." She rubbed her cigarette out on the step and turned to me. "Do you think of yourself as an angry person, Tom? Tell me the truth."

"No," I said. "I don't think so."

We sat there listening to the neighborhood.

"Your brother Alex was a lot like your sister," my mother finally said. *Your brother*, as a gentle reminder of our connection to each other. *Your sister*, as if Sue were as distanced from us now as Alex was. My mother could surprise me like that, by mentioning his name at odd times.

"He was always pushing himself," she continued, "the way she does. Except she gets frustrated sometimes and says things she doesn't really mean. I guess she has her father's temper.

But you're not like that, are you, Tom? You said that yourself. You're not an angry person." She leaned back and sighed, and I anticipated a small piece of advice coming my way, something I could apply to school or meeting friends.

"You can make use of even the worst circumstances," she told me. It was like my mother to look at adversity this way, as a chance for self-improvement, although she might have been trying to convince herself as much as me.

"What do you mean?" A light had come on in the downstairs window of the house across from ours—someone heading to the bathroom or letting out the dog.

"Oh, you know," she said, but she couldn't find more words. I seemed to watch her from some remote place, a point deep inside myself, the way children watch everything—with a scrutiny that has to pass as understanding. She looked off into the distance again, out across the yard and the neighborhood and the other end of town. "We should go to mass sometime," she said. "It was really beautiful there," and she laughed again, softly, as if she had said something ridiculous. Then she told me good night.

I stayed on the porch for what seemed like a long time after my mother had gone back to bed. When I was sure she was asleep I headed inside, opened the refrigerator, and poked around before heading upstairs to Alex's room. I often spent sleepless nights exploring that room, taking a *Popular Mechanics* down from the shelf or flipping through the record albums kept in milk crates lining the bottom of the closet. There were plastic army men on the dresser and sweaters folded neatly inside and six trophies for basketball and swimming arranged neatly on top of a set of high shelves, so that I had to stand on the bed to look at them.

Every year people in my town died young. But they died in groups. They died laughing and drunk, crashing their cars the night before the prom or diving from the cliff that overlooked the water-filled quarry at the edge of the city limits. Alex died alone, drowned in the public pond late one night. He was trying to make it to the other side, my mother told me—another test for himself. I was six years old when it happened, and I knew him mostly through my mother's stories and the things in his room, which my mother had left as they were when he died.

So I sat on Alex's bed and read a magazine. I looked over the strange, kaleidoscopic artwork on a record jacket. Eventually I turned back the bedspread and crawled underneath, where I unzipped my jeans and nestled my hand inside and then tried to sleep. In an hour I would get up, make the bed as carefully as possible, and find my way back to my room. Those days seem calm and almost motionless to me now, but there was a movement to them that was surprising, like the shimmer of a fish just beneath the water's surface. You catch it out of the corner of your eye—only for a second—and wonder if it was there at all.

Harris Fencer arrived in our lives during that summer before my sister's last year of high school, after my first year of middle school. We did not have many visitors in those days. When we did they were middle-aged men I knew from hardware stores or banks around town. They stayed over at the house once or twice, and I never saw them again except behind their counters and cash registers. Harris Fencer was different, although not in the way I first thought.

Before that summer I had known Harris only from the vending truck he drove around town. I often saw him at the stadium selling sandwiches wrapped in cellophane and sodas that weren't quite cold enough. He usually asked me how my mother was doing, and I told him she was fine, and I thought that was the extent to which our lives would intersect. So it felt strange when he started coming to dinner a couple of times a week and taking my mother out on Saturday nights. Sometimes he mowed our lawn or trimmed our hedges. When he came to the house he made a point of sitting me down and talking to me for a minute or two. Man-to-man chats, my mother called them.

He told me about how shy he was when he was a kid. Painfully shy, he called it, and he explained what he meant by example—stories about him roaming the outskirts of school dances and cringing in the back of classrooms. Then he would sigh, glance at his watch, put his hands on his knees, and stand with a groan. "Never get old," he said, though he didn't look that old to me, well into middle age maybe, a few years older than my mother.

I felt sorry for him, because he seemed uncomfortable around me. When I was serious, he laughed, and when I tried to make a joke, he didn't seem to understand. "I think there's something wrong with me," I told Sue. "I think I make Mr. Fencer nervous." We were throwing a softball back and forth in the yard.

"Cut it out," she said. "He was born nervous. It has nothing to do with you."

"I don't like him," I said, although that wasn't really true.

She looked hard at me then. Any small thing was enough to make her stop talking to me. For a second I thought I had crossed that invisible line again, and I was waiting for her to head inside when she said, "I don't like him either. He's always asking me all these dumb questions. He reminds me of a game show host." She placed her finger over her lip in imitation of his mustache and smiled a clenched grin. I made myself laugh, encouraging her to continue. Sometimes if I nudged her mood in the right direction she did impressions of our mother: the quick walk like she was always in a hurry, the flutter in the voice.

"Did you hear about the trophy case at school?" she asked. She was still smiling, as if she were telling a joke. I tried imagining the photograph of Alex. It had hung at the center of that case since I could remember, the state basketball championship trophy from his sophomore year on one side, a track-and-field award on the other.

"No," I said, which was also not true.

"Well, it was vandalized."

"Really?"

"Yes."

"I wonder who it was."

She looked at her feet, the ball in her hand. "I don't understand you," she said, and I nodded as if I didn't understand myself either, and then she threw the ball, hard this time. It sailed past me to the right. I heard it clatter against the fence. I backpedaled and found it in the dirt at the edge of the yard. When I turned to toss it back, Sue had moved in closer. She crouched and opened her glove at me. "I understand why you're mad," she said, "but if anyone has a right to be pissed off it's me." She glanced at the house like she wondered if someone was listening.

I threw the ball to her, and she took a step to her left and caught it, then opened and closed her glove, shifted her weight from foot to foot, mannerisms I had seen her use on the field when the mood of the game was turning for the worse. I remember thinking *she doesn't want to be here right now with me, in this house, this town.* It suddenly seemed possible that she would be gone tomorrow or the week after. "I'm doing my best," I said. "We're all doing our best." It was something I heard my mother say sometimes, defending me or Sue or someone on the television.

Sue laughed, looking down, her hands on her hips. She stood like this for what seemed like a long time until I was almost ready to step forward and touch her on the shoulder as a reminder that I was there. When she spoke again her voice was quiet, almost reverent. "I don't know if you should call it a lie if the person telling it believes it, but it's not the truth either, that's for sure. That's what you should know about Mom. She has this way of looking at things." She took a deep breath. Maybe she was getting ready to go inside. Maybe she had more to say. Almost by accident we found ourselves on the verge of something important.

This is when Harris Fencer appeared from around the hedges that separated our yard from the street. He held a brown grocery bag packed with what I knew was a change of clothes. "Hey," he said. I wondered how long he had been there, what he had heard. He stood waiting for us to start throwing the ball back and forth again, which we did two or three times before Sue said, "I have to go," and started walking toward the house.

"It's a nice evening," he said to me.

"It is," I said as if I had noticed it just then.

He glanced at the back porch screen door, which would not close unless it was forced. "I'll have to fix that," he said. "You can help if you want."

"That sounds good."

He rubbed the bridge of his nose where his glasses left small red marks. "I don't think your sister likes me much," he finally said. "In fact I know she doesn't. And that's okay, for now at least. But you should tell her that I'm as uncomfortable as she is. Maybe more." He smiled. "This is a strange situation to be coming into, you know."

I pictured my brother's trophies and magazines, the bed that was stripped and remade every few weeks along with the others, and I could see what he meant. It made me feel pleased and frustrated at the same time, I think, to have learned something but to have taken so long to learn it. "I'm glad it's finally summer," I said, although I didn't particularly care. I thought of it as an even trade, the small frustrations of school for summer's boredom.

"I bet," he said and laughed as if remembering when he was my age, some part of himself he wanted to see in me. "You know, I'm going to be around a lot more from now on." He was still looking over at the house, where my mother was most likely making dinner. He said it in a hushed voice like he was sharing a secret with me, something best kept from her. "Luck is a funny thing," he said, and he turned toward the street where a car was driving slowly by, the driver watching us—a father and son throwing a baseball around. "I mean, who would have guessed?" I think he wanted something from me, maybe just a simple nod of the head, the word *yes*. But I didn't want to give these things to him.

My mother had come out on the porch. I noticed her at the edge of my vision looking at the two of us as we talked, and I suddenly saw myself through her eyes—as a son perched precariously on the edge of her life, someone who needed a person like Harris Fencer as much as she did. I tried to imagine the shattering of glass, the handles of trophies snapped off, gold paint chipped to show white plastic underneath. I liked imagining myself swinging that make-believe bat, closing my eyes and feeling the ripple of contact move through the wood and into my body.

Summers in that part of the country then did not seem to lengthen so much as deepen. You could feel yourself moving down into them, losing sight of what had come before and what would come after, and pretty soon you were thinking that the days would always be that hot, and that slow, and that empty and perfect. Sue had begun lifeguarding part-time at a public pool, and when she was not working there, she was visiting one of her friends who also worked there, or at least that's what she told my mother. Sometimes she would not come home until the next morning. I would walk downstairs and see her eating from the open fridge, a chicken wing maybe and a glass of orange juice. She would see me in the doorway, say hello, and then bump the fridge door closed with her hip.

Harris and my mother spent their evenings buying things. I remember the crinkle of bags from the kitchen when they returned from shopping. They bought red-flowered plants that they hung from hooks in front of the windows so the neighbors could see them, and they bought clothes for my mother, which she held up for me to see. They bought lawn furniture, which they assembled in our yard, my mother reading the directions and laughing. On Saturday mornings the three of us sat around the shaky plastic table drinking lemonade or apple juice.

It was on one of these Saturdays at the end of July when my mother came into my room and said, "Would you like to go for a drive with me?" She looked tired, and she wore one of Sue's baseball caps—something I had never seen her do before. I didn't want to go, but there was something plaintive in the way she asked me, and so I followed her to the car and drove the thirty minutes out to what Harris Fencer called his old apartment. "Thanks for coming along," she said, when we were outside of town and there was no longer much of anything to look at. "I don't think this will take long. Just moving a few boxes. Harris says his friend, his ex-roommate, will be out there too, so we'll have some help."

"Sure," I said as I watched the trees and scrub slide by, the occasional half-hidden house.

"I worry about your sister," my mother said after a while. It seemed like something to fill the silence, but it was serious too. I could hear it in her voice.

"I know," I said.

"I really worry," she said again, as if she were trying to convince me. "She could make something of herself." I don't know what I thought about that. Maybe I agreed with her and that was all. Maybe the words pinched at me a little. I do know that didn't seem possible for me—to make a lot of myself the way Sue might at some invisible point in her future, or even to hurt those around me the way she seemed to be doing.

I don't remember much of the rest of the drive, although we talked about other things and laughed hard at a story my mother told, I forget which one. What I do remember is the man who met us at the top of the driveway where the pavement turned to dirt. He rested his hands on the window and leaned close, so that I could see his face clearly. He was smiling, and he had a sliver of something black in the corner of his mouth. One eye was partly closed and bloodshot, and although he was smiling, he looked like he was in pain.

"We're here for the last few things," my mother said, and she returned his smile.

"You'll have to park here," he said. "I wouldn't want you to get a flat." He took a step back from the car and looked down the stretch of dirt that led to the A-frame, and he smiled more, as if at some funny little fault in the world, and shook his head. "I'm going to have a grader come in some time and get rid of all the rocks, but for now it's not much of a driveway."

By the house two derelict cars sat on cinder blocks and a canoe rested upside down on sawhorses. At one end of the canoe, set back so I almost didn't notice, was a large doghouse with a chain trailing from inside to a stake in the ground about ten feet away. I didn't see a dog or hear one, and the water bowl near the house was overturned and covered with dirt, but I figured there was probably a dog somewhere, either up in the house or at the hidden end of that chain.

"Couldn't come out here himself," the man said when we had parked and I was opening up the back of the station wagon. It was like he was talking to himself but loud enough so we could hear.

"He told me to tell you," my mother said, "that he'll take care of everything. You'll have to give him a month or so is all."

"A month?" the man said and laughed.

"That's what he said."

"Well, I shouldn't even be getting into this, but you can tell him that he can forget the whole thing. It's not worth that much to me, to have it keep dragging on this way."

We walked up a narrow stairway built onto the front of the house and stepped into a refinished attic with small windows at either end. A path of light cut the room in half. Two chairs, a coffee table, and a few boxes had been piled together at the center of the floor. I noticed a narrow stove and sink—what looked like an afterthought. We lifted a chair and carried it out, my mother stepping backward down the stairs. The man lit a cigarette, then seemed to think better of it, because he rubbed it out on the windowsill and lifted one of the boxes, walking down after us. His eye, I realized, was an injury from long ago.

The second chair was larger and more difficult to carry, but we managed to get it downstairs. "That's right, Tom," my mom said as we moved down the steps. Then I was the one walking backwards, occasionally propping up the weight with a knee when we paused on a step. "Two more to go," she encouraged.

When we had loaded in the second chair she told me to wait by the car and then went back up the stairs. I looked around the property and wondered how long Harris had lived out here and what promises had been broken. I didn't know where the man had gone. He'd set the box on the ground by the car and vanished, but the dog had appeared in the corner of the yard and was watching me with serious curiosity.

A minute later the man appeared near the doghouse and, without acknowledging the dog, walked over and stood by the car, as if the three of us were going to drive off together when my mother came out of the house. "You know," he said, "I don't want to give you advice." He looked at the things in the car, and I could tell he was waiting for me to say something, although I figured it was best to say nothing at all. None of the things in our car seemed especially valuable or even nice, and I don't know why my mother would have gone to the trouble, except that she knew about the importance of even trivial things, how they accumulated history and meaning. Possibly they were important to Harris, and because of that maybe they were important to her. And maybe she thought she simply had a right to them.

She stepped out onto the upper landing holding a large brightly colored lamp, moving carefully, sliding her pointed toes across the edge of the step. She looked older then, and fragile, because of the way she was walking. The man met her on the stairway. I didn't hear what he said to her, but I heard how she replied. "Harris told me to get it," she said. I walked to the foot of the stairs, watching from a safe distance.

"That's not his, lady," he said. "It's the two chairs and the boxes. The coffee table isn't really his either, but I was trying to be nice."

"He said it was his," she said, and she took another step down, so that they were almost touching. I wished then that she wasn't holding the lamp, that the man had intervened sooner, or she had acted later. If it was still upstairs it would have been easy for us to leave. But she had it in her hands, and she was most of the way down the stairs now, and I think there was something about turning around that bothered her. Since then I have thought about it often, and what I saw as sentimentality in that moment could as easily have been tenacity. Standing the way she was, one step above him, made them look about the same height.

He put his hand on the lamp. For a moment it looked like he was going to say, *fine, take it*—that the touch was his way of saying good-bye—but his grip tightened and so did my mother's, and somehow they reversed positions, and he was suddenly above her. The struggle reminded me of grade-school fights I had seen but never been part of—some awkward pushing and grunting and bluster. I did nothing, although I think most people's instincts would have been to act, had they been seeing what I was seeing. But I remember thinking how ridiculous she looked, fighting over something like that with someone like him. And when he pulled the lamp away so that she stumbled and fell, I still didn't do anything except to take a single step forward.

She was on the ground then, gripping her shoulder, and the man stared at the lamp for a few seconds as if trying to figure out what he held in his hand. Then he threw it down the stairs. It hit the ground to one side of her and shattered, far enough away that I knew he had not meant to strike her. "I guess I didn't want either of us to have it," he said, and his voice was calm and almost regretful. But I don't think my mother heard him. She stood and sort of shuffled away. I watched her go. Her walk grew slower, more deliberate, and by the time she reached the car she had straightened up, and it was hard to tell that she had fallen at all. She was starting the car engine as I climbed in. At the top of the driveway she stopped and looked both ways carefully before taking the turn.

I thought of my brother reaching the middle of the pond—that moment where the distance behind him equaled the distance ahead and all his choices meant the same thing.

We did not speak for most of the ride home. She tuned the radio from station to station, and sometimes she hummed softly, then grinned in apology as if to say, allow me this small thing. It was a cool, relaxed smile, and it made me feel that everything would be fine.

"Do you want to stop for something to eat?" she asked when we were a few miles from home. The trees had given way to clusters of trailers and houses with dirt driveways. We had just passed a Dairy Queen, and we were taking a left onto the main drag.

"No," I said. "That's okay."

I think I didn't want to do anything to break the rhythm of that comfortable ride. I put my face close to the open window and watched the asphalt slide beneath us. It would not have bothered me if we had glided past our house and out through the other side of town, up to the hills and the interstate, where the land became thick with trees again. "We're here," my mother said as we pulled into the driveway.

I put my hand on the car door handle, and she put her hand on my knee and said, "Thomas, I'm pretty sure now what's going to happen, and let me tell you in advance that I'm sorry. I know what I said to you before, but I don't think Harris is going to be around much longer. I can tell even while I'm doing all this." And she looked behind her at the things we had gathered and then ahead, and she smiled as if she noticed something ridiculous out the windshield, in the architecture of the house, our lives. "Sometimes," she said, "plans don't work out the way we want them to. But even then they work out. We realize that later."

Harris met us on the second floor, his hair wet from a shower and a toothbrush in his hand. "How did it go?" he asked, and my mother said, "Fine. It went fine." She walked past him to the window where she pulled the curtains closed with a quick flip. "Just don't ask me to do something like that again."

Harris turned to me, smiled a light smile, and said, "Your mother is a good woman. She puts up with a lot. She's an angel really." Then he laughed and shook his head. With his chest bare, hair wet and falling around his face, he looked like a different person—funny and frightening at the same time—and I wondered if he knew this, if he could see himself that clearly.

"Harris is in a strange mood, Tom," my mother said. "It's best to ignore him."

"Your mother's right, Tom," he said. "It's best to ignore me. You should listen to your mother. She has experience with strange men."

I looked at him then—the sneer that a second ago I had mistaken for a smile, the way his eyes moved from her to me and then back again—and decided that he wasn't crazy at all, that he wasn't even as dangerous as he wanted to appear. He was just someone who was disappointed with himself and the way things were going. Turning away, I walked down the hall, running my hand along the wallpaper until I reached Alex's room, where I stopped, fingers resting against the doorframe. Most of his things, including the bed and bookcase, had been moved out, and the open space held me motionless. Behind me Harris was putting on his shoes. In a minute he'd walk quickly downstairs and out to his truck and pull out of the driveway and down the street, and then I'd ask my mother a question, because she would be standing behind me, waiting for me to ask that question.

"Where do you think he is right now?"

That's what I finally said when my mother appeared behind me. I was thinking of Harris driving his truck out along the route we had just traveled. Maybe he was heading back to that house in the woods. She seemed to think for a second and then she said, "Oh, he's in a good place," because she had misunderstood who I was asking about.

And I wasn't sure if I was thinking of Harris anymore either. It seemed such an easy thing to do—to let him slip from my mind—although he was still in there somewhere, mixed up with my father and brother. "Do you think we're anything alike?" I asked without really knowing whom I was talking about now. I wanted to be like somebody, I suppose, and the particulars of that person didn't matter so much.

My mother waved her hand dismissively at my question. The gesture wasn't angry, or even annoyed, but matter-of-fact, as if this were a pointless thing to think about. "Oh, worlds apart," she said, and I wanted to ask her something else simply to keep the words flowing, but nothing came to mind. "We'll talk more tomorrow," she said, although we didn't, not about that, or the car ride that afternoon, or the brief time when Harris Fencer lived under our roof.

Once I asked my mother where my father lived, and she told me Baton Rouge. He had moved there a couple of years before Alex died, she said, although she did not use the word *move*, she used the word *wandered*.

I can picture my father becoming a different person in Louisiana, his skin tanning, his accent softening in his mouth. I can imagine the kinds of things he was trying to free himself from. "I've never been there," she said, "but I bet it's fantastic." And then suddenly we were talking about other beautiful places she had never been—Spain, San Francisco, Nova Scotia, Colorado. I have been to some of those places since and although I'm happy to have seen them, I don't think they were as beautiful as the images my mother must have carried around in her imagination. I live in Portland, Oregon, now, and I sometimes wonder if my mother thinks my life here is an exotic one.

Despite the distance, I've tried to keep in touch with my family. I haven't visited them in years—I can't afford to—but I try to call whenever I have news to tell, which isn't that often. Sue is married and living in Miami with a man I have never met. She puts her children on the extension whenever we speak, their happy nonsense talk a thin barrier between us. My mother still lives in the same house, and when we talk she tells me mild news about the neighborhood, the weather, and her health. Which is why it was so surprising when she brought him up last week. For a moment I had no idea what she was talking about.

"Remember that ice cream man?" she asked, and then she began to tell me.

"Hold on one second," I said. I had been washing last night's dinner dishes as we talked, the phone in the crook of my neck, and I shut off the water, turned my back to the sink, and dried my hands.

Harris Fencer had been dead for a long time—almost five years—and so it felt strange to hear as news what anybody else who may have cared would already have forgotten. She had found out herself only a few months before, from an old friend she had bumped into somewhere. Her voice had the assured and detached tone of someone who had taken a good amount of time deciding exactly how to repeat the story. I slid a chair over from the kitchen table, sat down, and tried hard to be attentive.

"It wasn't the best of circumstances" is how she put it. The police had found him in an abandoned cabin where he must have been squatting, dead from a heart attack, although my mother implied that something shady had been involved. I realized then that she was talking about Harris Fencer in the same way that she had once talked about my father. As a kind of accident, I think, as something that simply happens to you.

"Why don't you call Sue about this?" I said. "You talk to her all the time."

"I thought you would want to know," she said. "You and I, we shared this. This was ours, Tom."

"Our secret," I added.

"You don't understand," she said, and her voice broke, and suddenly we were talking about something else. "You don't know how difficult it was," she said. "You don't have any idea," and her voice quavered. "I have a right to be happy, don't I?"

I didn't hear anything else—not even her breathing—and for a moment I thought she might have hung up. Then she sniffled and cleared her throat and I felt like I should tell her something, although I didn't know what that thing was, or even if it would be gentle or cruel. So I didn't say a thing except that I really had to go. I broke the line with a push from my thumb. Still holding the phone in my hand, I thought of the dog watching us, my mother's words in the car, the two of us walking that dead man's belongings into the house. The memories resurfaced with such velocity and clarity that I almost dialed my mother's number again, although I still had no idea what to say. It is a difficult story to talk about—especially with the person who shared it with me.

Maybe I would have begun with the part she doesn't know.

I remember waking late that night with my leg and shoulder pushed against my bedroom wall. My palm pressed flat against the wall too, like I was trying to find a heartbeat. I didn't know what had woken me, but I heard voices from in front of the house, Sue and someone else. I thought I heard a can hitting the pavement and then laughter. I pushed myself up and scuffed across the floor in my socks.

My mother's door was ajar, and I noticed on the way past that her bed was made except for one corner, where the blankets had been pulled down in a small fold. A plate with a half-eaten hot dog and some potato chips had been left on one of the pillows. I noticed one of the boxes we had moved that day overturned on the floor, empty.

I seemed to float downstairs and through the house until I reached the front door and stepped outside. Sue was sitting on the hood of the car. When she saw me she raised her hand and waved with her fingers as if she had been expecting me. "Bobby, this is my little brother Tom," she said and smiled at the boy beside her. He was tall and thin in a way that seemed almost unhealthy. He leaned against the car drinking a beer, trying hard not to look interested.

"We're just saying goodnight," she said to me. "Bobby has to get up early tomorrow . . . I guess that's today," she laughed, "a couple of hours from now."

I noticed then that my mother's car was not there. The truck was parked in its usual place in our narrow driveway, the passenger's side tires on the lawn.

"Tom's had an interesting day," she said to Bobby. "He was with my mother this afternoon. She asked him to go with her." She smiled, and her voice grew high and agitated. She was imitating my mother now. "She needed some support. She needed help." I couldn't tell if the hysteria in her voice was all mocking, or if part of it was genuine, and I didn't care. I just wanted her to stop. Although she didn't have a bottle in her hand, I could tell she had been drinking.

A car appeared a few blocks up the street and moved toward us. Bobby stepped back and put the hand holding the beer inside the window of his car until the other vehicle passed by. All I could see was soft red taillights moving away from us.

"Bobby's paranoid," Sue said. "Bobby's not nearly as dangerous as he thinks he is."

He shrugged as if he knew this long before Sue did. "It sounds like it's your mother who's the crazy one," he said.

"I didn't say you were crazy, honey," she said, cooing artificially at him as she touched his shoulder. "I just said you were paranoid."

"I still want to see his room," he said. "Nobody's home. Let's go. Unless you think it's too creepy." He stretched out this last word into one slow syllable, *creeeepy*, and wiggled his fingers like claws.

Sue frowned and lifted herself off the hood and walked away a little, back turned to me. I was bracing myself for an insult or at least a command for me to head back inside. "Tom is home," she said.

"Whatever," Bobby said. "I just want to see his room."

"It's nothing special," I said. "It's just a room," and Sue gave me a dirty look.

"I know people like to talk about my brother," she said, turning to Bobby like he was the one who had spoken, "but we're not some kind of freak show. Tom is right. It's just a room."

"I didn't say you were a freak," he said.

"I don't think he and I understood each other very well," she went on. "He was close to my mother, but not that close, you know? She was closer to him than he was to her. I guess that's what I mean."

Bobby wasn't listening, but I was. "Was he like me?" I asked.

"Yes, I think so," she said, although maybe this was meant to make me feel better. Maybe she meant we were all alike, the men in my family, or men in general. I didn't know if I wanted that or not, even if it was true. She said, "You think things are crazy around here these days. The month before Alex drowned, that was crazy." She glanced away from me, at the house, at Bobby. "But as crazy as it was I didn't think he'd do what he did." And she stopped then, although I wanted her to go on.

Bobby walked over to her and put his hand on her shoulder. "It's okay," he said, and I realized he had been listening after all.

"I know," she said, and then they were quiet, as if some kind of understanding had been reached. I listened to the nighttime sounds—sparse traffic on the overpass moving softly as a river, crickets underneath it all. And then one sound grew louder than the rest, a single car moving up the street from behind us. We turned and I narrowed my eyes as the headlights slid across our bodies. Bobby stepped back to make room for it to pass, but I stayed where I was, and the car slid to one side and let out a long wail of its horn as it traveled the length of the street. Its brake lights flashed red at the intersection, and then it disappeared around the corner.

"Jesus," Sue hollered after them. "Lunatics." She spread her legs gunfighter style, both hands cupped to her mouth as she yelled, and when she lowered her arms and turned back to me she was grinning. "So I answered your questions," she said. "Now you have to tell me about your day. What was Mom so upset about tonight?"

There are the things that happen to us. And there are the things we could say about them. I knew then that my mother would probably never tell Sue anything about that trip we took, and especially not about those hard little facts that had stood out so clearly to me—the damp smell of the house, the struggle on the stairs, her hobble back to the car. I said, "You should have seen it. It was pretty funny."

"Oh?" she asked, and I hesitated. But then I began to tell her.

CODE

My office did not look like my office. I had asked the department secretary to redecorate it while I was on vacation, and she had filled it with hanging plants — spidery things with long sharp leaves. All the green made me nervous. The increased feeling of responsibility depressed me. The plants would die and it would be my fault. Still it was good to be back, better than being at home where life's only choices seemed to be the noise of the television or a serene suburban quiet that made me feel like something horrible was going to happen.

When I had parked my Explorer in its familiar reserved space that morning, I felt relief, more than anything else, to be back where I belonged. I had even worn a new shirt — blue gray to match my steely resolve — and polished my best shoes. The sun was strong and high in the east as I walked to the building, and a cluster of little birds hopped around the parking lot mechanically pecking at the grit near the empty handicapped spaces.

My travel thermos still contained half a cup of surprisingly good coffee. If I wasn't full of love for any particular individual, I was at least spilling over with good feeling for mankind in general. Living seemed a good idea.

"You look great," the security guard at the front desk said as I signed in. The day before, I had sprawled out on a lawn chair in the yard for a couple of hours so I'd have a healthy glow.

"Where did you go?" he asked. I wondered if I had just returned from a better vacation than I had imagined.

"Europe," I said in an attempt to be impressive and ambiguous at the same time.

"Europe," he said thoughtfully. With one word I had opened a gap between us, a distance he could be amazed by or get indignant about, depending on his mood.

"Yes," I said. "Next year I'm planning to go to Asia."

"Wow," he said, "that would be something," and he turned around the logbook and inspected my signature as if looking for a clue to my success in the fat curves of my name.

Guldeck and Cranlan met me at the elevator. "Hey," Guldeck said. "If it isn't you." He pointed at me with a thick finger, holding the elevator door for the crowd—tastefully dressed people who looked something like me. They sprayed the same juices under their arms and worried about the same things when they looked in a mirror at three in the morning. Except—and this was a crucial difference—they were not me, were they? Sometimes I didn't even feel like me.

As we jockeyed for position and I smelled their colognes and perfumes and aftershaves, it passed through my mind that maybe someone in the crowd could be better at being me than I had been. Then I thought of my empty house with its cheese-encrusted pizza boxes and half-empty photo albums and realized that someone out there right now was probably doing just that.

"I thought you weren't due back until next week," Guldeck said. He was a large, excitable man who had a way of making those around him feel rushed. Often I had heard people complain about how they couldn't think straight in proximity to him. He had the rough hands of a construction worker, someone who spent his time gripping and lifting.

"That's true," I said, "but some issues came up with a particular project. Things I had to address personally."

"No substitute for the hands-on approach," Cranlan said, and he laughed quietly as if disdaining such a simple idea. He did this often, I noticed—summarized someone else's words with a subtly sarcastic chuckle, a study in economy and control, a barely audible noise that could make you feel inadequate at a near-childish level. I would have added the technique to my repertoire if Cranlan had not mastered it so completely that it seemed inseparable from him.

The elevator reached the fourth floor, the crowd reshuffled, and the three of us pushed into the hallway. "You should know," Guldeck said. "We have a situation."

"It's another reorganization, Michael," Cranlan said. "I haven't seen it, but there's a list of names going around, circulating at the top levels."

"A list," I said.

"Exactly right," he said.

"Of the soon-to-be dead and wounded."

"We've missed your flair for the dramatic, Michael."

We entered the company's executive kitchenette, where we stood around the lunch table. I knew each of us was wondering who would be the first to reach for the tray of pastries at its center, giving up his self-control and enabling the rest to do the same. Guldeck opened the microwave and scraped at a brown splotch with his pen. "I've been dreaming about that list, you know. But I can't read the words."

I picked up a small circular roll with a swirl of gray-purple at its center and held it out to Guldeck. "Relax," I said. "Have something to eat." He eyed the pastry suspiciously.

"Damn it," he said. "Is it too much to ask to get a decent raspberry Danish? Where do they get this stuff?" He began to lift and inspect various pastries, looking them over with contempt. Cranlan was now picking apart a chocolate doughnut as a way to avoid eating it. A habit of his, I had noticed, his own nervous way to keep trim. Each day he left a pile of doughnut rubble behind for the cleaning crew to throw away.

"Whose responsibility is this?" Guldeck asked. He pointed his thumb over his shoulder at the wall behind him. "What's-her-name? I bet it's what's-her-name. She should be the first one to get the chop-chop."

"No," I said. "Not her."

Guldeck said, "I was in at seven yesterday. To get a head start on the day, you know? And I still didn't get a raspberry one. The tray was out here, but the raspberry ones were gone."

"Maybe there weren't any to begin with."

"Bullshit. I know they exist. I've seen people walking around eating them. I've seen you walking around eating them." A fleck of spittle had formed on his lip, shimmering as he talked.

Cranlan smiled. "I bet they were enjoying themselves, these hypothetical people with their hypothetical pastries."

"Considerably," Guldeck said. "Much more than I am right now eating this fossil." He set it back on the edge of the tray, two bites out of the side. Cranlan picked it up and tore it in half, scrutinized its dark and moist underside, which looked like some light-sensitive mollusk.

"Have a lemon-filled," I said. "They're okay."

"I don't want okay, Michael. I don't think I should have to settle for okay. I Stairmaster for forty-five minutes every night just so I can get away with eating this kind of stuff, and I definitely want it to be better than okay."

We stood there studying the small mound at the center of the table, amazed at its architecture. Then we pulled away one by one, and I went to my office and tried to ignore the plants. After about three minutes of staring at paperwork, I picked up the phone and punched in the extension for building supply. As the phone rang on the other end somewhere in the bowels of the building, I took a seat on the corner of my desk in the attitude of a man accomplishing things.

"Hello," I said. "Natalie?" It was Natalie. I had forgotten how good it was to hear her voice, and I forgave her instantly for not returning the calls I had made to her home phone during the last couple of weeks. "I have a question for you," I continued. "I'd like some new furniture for my office. I was thinking about an uncomfortable chair. Simple and traditional. I need to feel stoic."

"We just sent you a new chair two weeks ago," Natalie said.

I looked around my office — the bookcase littered with books abandoned by its previous occupant, the three teal-colored file cabinets along the back wall, the imported Indian carpet my wife and I had bought what seemed like years ago. I saw no such chair.

"And by the way, Michael. You said you had a question. What just came out of your mouth wasn't a question. It was a statement. People are always calling me up and telling me they have a question, but what they really should say is they'd like to make a statement."

"I'm sorry. I don't want to be part of your problems, Natalie. I want to be part of the *solution* to your problems."

"Why do you need this chair? What are you doing that's so important it demands that I drop everything and rush a chair over to you?"

"I have my fingers in a lot of different pies right now."

"Because I hate to say this, but I've heard rumors."

She was referring to the memo of course, and my subsequent absence from the office. The memo had appeared one day in my employee mailbox, folded authoritatively across the middle and signed by a vice president of something important sounding. It explained in simple, tersely affectionate language that the entire company would be more or less hibernating for most of June and this would be an ideal opportunity for me to get some much deserved downtime.

"I don't want to know," I told her, although I did. I had heard rumors too. The building throbbed with them.

"What are you working on these days?" she asked. "I mean, before your leave of absence. What were you working on?"

"Various things," I said. "Various important things. And it was a vacation. I went to Europe. But before Europe, before my vacation, I had my fingers in a lot of pies. This one project in particular keeps arriving on my desk. I add to it and then it comes back and I take stuff away."

"You're saying that its weight fluctuates."

"I'm saying that it has reached the pulsing stage. It is moving in and out. It's breathing. Like some kind of experiment from a horror movie."

"Frankenstein."

"The Blob."

"Whatever."

"Yeah. Whatever. It's around here somewhere. I expect to see it momentarily. Unless the plug has been pulled on the whole thing, which is a distinct possibility. As you know I'm a little removed from the process right now."

I lifted myself off the desk and walked to the window, where I played with my blinds, opening and closing them: small rhythms and repetitions, like an awkward attempt at semaphore. From my office I could sometimes see people in the next building. Ours was the nicer building, a full four stories taller, with a cafeteria on the ground floor.

"I'm wondering what the point of these conversations is," Natalie said. "People are beginning to talk."

"I see. A question of propriety. I have a corner office. You work in the supply room."

"That's right."

"The Capulets and the Montagues."

"Exactly."

"Regardless, I think you should go to lunch with me today. With a bunch of us. Safety in numbers. You can tell me what you've heard from the rumor mill. I'll buy you a drink, and I'll tell you the rumors I've heard."

"That's very nice of you," she said. I could tell she was interested in what I might know and afraid, too, should this information involve her. But she was too polite to say anything. I had noticed before that these two emotions—politeness and mild fear—seemed to charge the atmosphere in every corner of the building, like the buzz of fluorescence.

"What about my chair?" I asked her.

"That'll have to go through channels."

"Maybe I'll just buy a folding chair and bring it in."

"I wouldn't do that. You'd be stepping on some toes. Some very powerful toes. It's bad form for someone in your position."

"What is my position?"

"I'm not sure, but it's obviously essential."

"That's true," I said. "You know how when you were a kid and you asked your mom how the fridge or the car worked, and she said there were little men in there turning the gears?"

"I guess so."

"Well, I like to think of myself as one of those little men."

"I'm not sure what you mean," she said, "but I do know that a folding chair could be misconstrued."

I squeezed my lips with my left hand until they puckered. Sometimes when talking on the phone I found myself playing with my face, absorbed in the soft give of my skin.

"I have to go now," she said.

"Think about lunch," I said, and using two fingers killed the connection. I felt giddy, although I couldn't tell exactly why. I took a folder off my desk and skimmed the contents. Not much of it registered, other than the four neat columns of numbers, but it was something to keep my eyes and hands occupied as I paced the room.

I tried to get something accomplished, but I kept thinking about the blankets and pillows on my couch. I had left the lights on upstairs so that it would look like someone was home already when I drove up the street in the evening. The bed was unmade and had been for weeks, for months. Had it ever been made? This seemed to be an enormous problem, and the solution had been to sleep downstairs—on the couch, on the back porch, on the kitchen floor. I explored the house and touched my cheek to places it had never touched before. I suppose I was trying to find a way to relate. I was wondering if the house remembered me.

I had forgotten to flush the toilet. I was sure of it.

Through the closed door, I could hear the department secretary out there talking. "Yes, he's in," she was saying, "but you can't speak with him. He's brainstorming right now." I thought about playing racquetball or shooting hoops or harassing someone in the Midwest about a late package. I kicked off my shoes and flexed my toes. I loosened my tie and stretched, then did a couple of halfhearted deep knee bends.

Brainstorming. I liked the sound of that. It seemed to elevate my life to an exalted state, as if I were a quirky genius daydreaming of flow charts, brooding over a sliver-sized sixth decimal place. I took off my socks and slid my feet through the carpet. Then I balled up one sock and practiced throwing it at the wastebasket across the full width of the room, keeping count in my head.

The first shots went wide, the next three fell short, but the three after that entered the mouth of the can with a satisfying thump. I was bouncing from foot to foot but stopped to unbutton my shirt and slide my belt from around my waist and sling it over the back of my chair. I shot again, trying to release and retrieve the sock as fast as possible. My breathing grew heavy, and I bent over with my hands on my knees and inhaled through my nose in what I considered to be a virile way. I took time to snort and hawk and swallow. The back of my neck felt warm.

I took off my shirt and draped it on the chair with the belt, then retrieved the sock from the corner. It hit the wall to the right of the trash. I moved toward it on the floor but stopped halfway and went into reverse, unbuttoning my pants. I folded them on my desk. I filed my underwear in the bottom drawer where I kept empty folders and unopened office supplies.

Whenever the ball plopped into the basket, I pumped my fist and threw some left-right combinations at the air. I picked up the phone and punched the first extension that occurred to me, leaving the sock there in what had become its rightful place.

"Hello," someone said.

"Foster," I said.

"This is Schwartz."

"Exactly," I said, "just the man I want to talk to."

"Is that you, Michael?" he asked.

"It is I."

He snorted. "It's good to have you back."

"It's good to be back."

"What can I do you for?"

"Well, I was wondering if you'd heard."

"Heard what?"

"You know. The rumors."

"I have. I've heard different things from different people. Most of it seems pretty far-fetched."

"Regardless."

"You're breathing very heavily, Michael. I have a very obscene phone call kind of feeling going on here, you're breathing so hard. You wouldn't be having a heart attack?"

"Nothing like that," I said.

"Good," he said. "That's very good. I'm pleased to hear it."

"Can you reiterate what you've heard?" I asked him. "I'd like to match up my facts with your facts."

"It's a purge. Everyone knows. All departments. All levels.

The company is sticking its finger down its throat. Are you having lunch out today?"

I looked at my wall clock. It was almost time to eat.

Most of the tables at the restaurant were empty. The busboys had just begun setting places for lunch, and the waitresses were talking at the bar. I immediately felt reassured by the familiar particulars—the wide wooden chairs, heavy silverware, and thick cloth napkins of a good steak place.

I noticed one of the busboys, younger than the others. He moved from table to table, wiping away the red scab from around the lip of the ketchup bottles, filling the salt and pepper shakers. "We'd like a table," I told him when he got close, and he nodded and walked away holding his stained napkin.

"We're early," Schwartz said.

"It's never too early," I said.

We were whispering as if we had just entered a church between services. We moved to the center of the room, to our usual table. A waitress met us there.

"Your collar buttons are undone," Schwartz said.

"Thanks," I said and stood there fiddling.

A small man appeared at the entrance. He held the door open with his shoulder, not in and not out, and at first I thought he was going to turn around and leave, but then he saw us and waved, and we waved back.

"Barnes," Schwartz said. "Look at how short he is. I always forget how short he is."

"The strange thing is how he can find a suit that's a size too small when he's so small himself. It seems like you'd have to expend some real effort to do that."

We took turns shaking hands, then found our places. "I'll have a rum and Coke," I told the waitress as I pulled out my chair. "As strong as legally possible. Only a splash of Coke." I made a fanning gesture. "In fact just wave the Coke bottle over the glass. That'll do."

She looked at Barnes, then Schwartz. "The same thing," Schwartz said, "except with less Coke."

Barnes opened the menu, looked it up and down. "I'll have the chicken Parmesan and a ginger ale."

Schwartz leaned forward, both arms on the table. "We're just ordering drinks, Barnes."

I nodded. "Generally we order drinks, maybe some appetizers, then unwind for fifteen or twenty minutes. Then we order the food. Then we wait for the food, which is not an inopportune time to have another drink, and then we eat the food."

"Pacing is everything," Schwartz said.

By this time Guldeck and two people I didn't know had come in and dragged the nearest table over to ours, getting a couple of nervous stares from other patrons trickling in. As he sat down Guldeck reached across me for an ashtray. "Hear the latest?"

"No," I said.

"Accounting," he said, and he tapped the ashtray against the table in a staccato rhythm, as if clicking out Morse code. One of the people I didn't know drew his finger across his throat and made a sound like an incision. Then he looked at me and smiled as if I should know him. Guldeck was ordering drinks. He was ordering lots of drinks.

"I saw it coming," Schwartz said. "They've had their head up their collective ass for some time now."

Barnes pointed at me with his fork. "Speaking of which,

how's your particular project coming along? I heard a date had been set."

"They always do that," Schwartz said. "They set a date. They change the date. They change it again. Nothing is fixed. Don't worry about it." He slapped me on the shoulder.

I saw the waitress across the room, her tray loaded with glasses, moving toward us. I kept my eyes on hers as she narrowed the space. Something about the moment seemed peaceful, almost profound, and I did not want it to end. I held up my empty glass as a kind of hello. She closed the space between us with a few decisive steps and replaced it with a full one.

Guldeck was talking now. "That entire project has become our personal Viet Nam. We should just pull out and cut our losses." The waitress handed him a glass that seemed mismatched to the size of his hand. I wondered if he played football in college. He took a long sip and scowled into his lap. "You can feel good bourbon in your extremities. That's the main thing I look for."

He touched the waitress, holding her there as he emptied the glass. Then he handed it back to her. "Another round of the same. Bring everyone another of whatever they're having." Guldeck swept his hand, indicating the bunch of us.

A few more people were squeezing in around the table, and other waitresses had appeared with large plates of appetizers. Nachos and honey-glazed chicken wings. "I have an important meeting this afternoon, you know," Guldeck said to nobody in particular. "I have to balance my body chemistry."

I pulled one of the appetizer plates to me and tugged a steaming nacho loose from the coagulated cheese, taking careful bites. "You're preparing," I told him. "You're mentally girding your loins."

"That's what I'm doing. And that's what you should do too. I think Wassermann from marketing is sitting in on this thing, and you know how he can be."

That was the first I had heard of Cameron Wassermann being involved in that afternoon's meeting. And my own inclusion came as an even bigger surprise.

"Good luck," someone said, and small guttural agreements came from everyone.

When two waitresses appeared with more trays of drinks, I offered to buy the next round. It was something I figured I should do before more people arrived. The group was big enough now that the conversation had split into three or four huddles.

"Damn the youth of America to hell," someone was saying at the end of the table. Was it a joke? I wasn't sure.

Barnes was leaning over his plate, sawing his chicken into neat squares. "You know, I invested a lot of time in that project independent of anyone else," he said. No one but me seemed to hear him. By this time a dozen of us were clustered around three tables pushed end to end. Guldeck kept insisting on buying drinks for people and threatening to punch them if they refused. Someone suggested that we sing sea chanteys. It seemed in keeping with the overall mood.

Schwartz put his arm around my shoulder. "You know what I love?" he asked with real sincerity. "I love the atmosphere. There's this Last Supper kind of thing going on. That kind of feeling, you know? That kind of oh-my-God-what's-going-to-happen-next." He laughed and lifted his empty glass to his mouth.

"Please," I said. "No ironic observations."

"What's the matter?"

"Nothing. I guess I don't like your reference."

"To the Last Supper?"

"That's right. Crucifixion gives me the willies."

"The whole death thing."

"Yes. That's right. The whole death thing."

"The icy hand on your heart. The black void."

I turned to talk to the person on my left, but he was talking to the person on his left: something about how useless pennies were, like our pinkies, and we were evolving out of a need for either, and was it just a coincidence that the two words sounded so much alike?

I turned back to Schwartz. "I didn't go to Europe."

He straightened up and seemed to sober. "I know," he said, and as a smile crossed his face he suddenly looked drunk again.

"I hate vacations. All that being alone with yourself. All that contemplation. It's claustrophobic."

"Peeking into the coffin of yourself," he slurred softly, as if talking to himself. I noticed that he was eyeing my glass, so I slid it to him. He finished the drink for me and burped a thank you just as the next round was arriving.

"I can't stop thinking about that list," I said. Guldeck's words, sort of, but now they were mine. I looked over at him. He had an elbow on the table, open hand ready to grip and arm-wrestle the first taker. "I should go," I said. "I've been waiting for Natalie, but she's not going to show."

"Cranlan didn't make an appearance either."

"That's right. I wonder what happened to him?"

Schwartz shrugged, and we both stood. "Can you drive?" I asked him. He was listing toward one side as if he were standing on a bad leg.

"Not really," he said.

I threw some money at the center of the table. "Me neither."

"We'll flip a coin and cross our fingers," he said, and he took an awkward step toward the door. For some reason I was feeling pretty good again. Something inside me had shifted.

On the way out I collided with the busboy. Even though more than an hour had passed since I last saw him he was still hard at work cleaning ketchup bottles. One of them leapt from his hand as we crashed into each other. A streak of red splattered across my chest and I stood with my arms wide apart, looking down at my shirt. "I'm shot," I said and I staggered— although I didn't exactly mean to—and everyone laughed.

As soon as I got back to work I went by Cranlan's office and knocked on the doorframe. When nobody answered I stepped inside, moving deliberately, one hand on the wall for balance. Someone else sat behind Cranlan's desk, a small gray-haired man turning the pages of a pocket dictionary. Cranlan's bulletin board, which had previously been blank except for his business card tacked in one corner, was now covered with clippings from the comic pages: a confusion of boxes and word balloons. A squat minifridge stood in the corner in place of Cranlan's empty bookcase, a bowl of apples on top.

"Where's Cranlan?" I asked.

The man looked up, startled, watery eyed. "What?"

"Cranlan."

"Um."

"Never mind," I said, and I left.

Four or five people were gathered around the copy machine in the hall, pressing buttons, opening doors, peering inside. "Jammed," one of them said to me as if asking for help, but

I kept walking. I headed to the restroom, where I bent over the sink and splashed cold water on my face. From one of the stalls I could hear the gasps and spurts of someone violently upchucking.

I tried cleaning my shirt with a wet paper towel. The ketchup spread and faded to pink. A large pale stain didn't seem to be that much of an improvement over a small dark one, so I stopped scrubbing. Instead I tightened the knot of my tie, took my pen from my shirt pocket and clicked it in and out, in and out, something to keep my hands busy while I listened. The noise from the stall gradually subsided, and Guldeck appeared at the sink next to me, looking pale except for the top of his balding head, which glowed baby red. We both stood there looking into the mirror. "Damn," he said. He took a small bottle of mouthwash from his pocket and began to gargle and spit.

I spoke to his reflection. "You've heard about Cranlan, I assume."

He swished, puffing one cheek, then the other.

"We can't afford to be sentimental, obviously," I said.

He tilted his head back, leaned forward, and dribbled green liquid into the sink. When he was finished he took hold of his lips and curled them back so he could inspect his teeth. "You know," he said, "something about the suddenness of these things seems correct. Almost Darwinian. It's like watching one of those nature documentaries."

"It's like itself," I said. I had pulled off my tie and was unraveling the knot, starting from scratch. "That's what it reminds me of. When I first came in this morning I looked around and took a deep breath and said to myself, 'This reminds me of being back at the office.'"

Guldeck was halfway to the door. He turned around, walking backward, and raised his fist in salute. "Onward and upward." The door closed behind him, and I turned back to the mirror. Guldeck would be gone by the end of the week, I realized, once some higher-up understood the incongruity of having him walking around without Cranlan, his opposite number, yin to his yang, Laurel to his Hardy. I picked up his forgotten bottle of mouthwash and put it in my pocket.

I followed him into the hall, where we moved in separate directions. I glanced repeatedly at my watch without really noticing what time it was, a reflex action that made me look determined and efficient. Or nervous and fixated, either or both, I didn't know. I was holding my tie in both hands now, stretched taut like a garrote. I had no idea what time the tele-conference began. I could have been twenty minutes late or an hour early. I stopped, trying to orient myself.

Someone I didn't know pointed down the hall. "It's that way," he said, but how did he know what I was looking for? And who was he anyway? "Right," I said, although I didn't move. The floor swayed beneath me in a soft ripple like the wake from a passing boat. Then with a surge of will that seemed almost superhuman I began to walk in the direction he had pointed.

Cameron Wassermann shook my hand at the door, then stepped aside and waved his arm dramatically, motioning me to enter. He wore a loud Hawaiian-print T-shirt, untucked around his ballooning waist. His Docksiders were untied. I almost expected him to be holding a glow-in-the-dark tropical drink. There were two types of salespeople, I had decided long ago: the hungry younger ones, moving toward vague vice presi-dencies and company cars, and the spent older ones, moving toward retirements and multiple strokes. Cam was deep into the latter group.

"Michael," he said, "you look like absolute hell."

"Thanks."

"How was your vacation? I heard that you went to Europe."

"Yes."

"Did you like it?"

"Loved it."

"And your wife and kids?"

"I loved them too," I said, and we both laughed, although at different jokes. He was still double-gripping my fist. I wanted it back.

Still laughing, he grabbed Guldeck by the wrist and pulled him over to us. "Michael, I'd like you to meet Ken Guldeck, our director of . . ." He turned to Guldeck, voice trailing off.

"Intercorporate Situations," Guldeck said.

"Director of Intercorporate Situations," Wassermann said, and the smile returned to his wide sun-dried face. I shook Guldeck's hand vigorously.

"Pleased to meet you," I said. "You have quite the reputation." It seemed strange to be talking to someone who would likely end up as a casualty. The feeling was there as I shook his hand—the sense of being close to extinction and not wanting it to rub off on you.

"Sorry I'm late," Barnes said as he came through the door. He was wiping his forehead with his handkerchief, a gentle, cultivated gesture that made me want to grab him in a headlock. "I was moving Schwartz's computer over to my office," he said. "You should see the programs he has on that thing. Versions of software that haven't even been released yet. He must have had some contacts."

"The past tense," I said.

"That's right," Wassermann said. "You didn't hear?"

"No," I said.

"They canceled his passwords about an hour ago. He can't access a thing. If he put change in the candy machine, it would pop out the coin return."

I crossed Schwartz's name off the list that was floating somewhere in the back of my mind. We moved to sit down around the table, where blank pads of paper and pencils with new points were set at each place.

"Take a second," Wassermann said. "Get your heads in order. Visualize an optimal situation an hour from now maybe, once we've done what we have to do." He had started eating a Danish from who knows where, and he was licking sugar glaze from his fingers. I suppressed the urge to lift a pencil like a dagger and hurl myself across the table. My heart was a sieve and my negative emotions were dirty water.

I pictured a room in San Francisco with four people much like us sitting around a table much like ours, a balance that seemed important, even essential: two groups at either end of the country, arranged with the beautiful symmetry of Greek pillars or tensed football teams. That was the main satisfaction, I think, in a meeting like this. Yelling and hearing the echo of your words come back to you, the connectedness of those disembodied voices haggling and joking and coming to agreement.

Wassermann clicked the speakerphone button at the center of the table. We made the introductions, eight names and titles. At that moment it seemed that whatever happened in the next hour would resound with the clarity of something that mattered. I wanted to drop to the floor and do push-ups. I wanted to double over and be sick. That feeling always passed over me just before a meeting, only for a moment or so, before time seemed to catch and move forward again, like a skipped cog.

"Have you looked at the demo?" Wassermann asked.

"Excuse me?" asked the voices on the speakerphone.

"The demo," Barnes said. "Have you had a chance to look at it?" He raised his voice and enunciated each syllable. "You know. The demo we mailed you." As he repeated himself the word seemed to recede, becoming hazy and vague like music playing in another room.

I took a pad of paper and wrote, "It's like he's visiting his grandfather in the rest home." I slid it over so Guldeck could read it. He smiled and nodded, scratched something back.

"Axed," it said. Next to the word he drew what he probably intended to be a small axe, although it didn't look much like one. I turned the page and drew a large question mark.

"Effective Friday," he wrote in jagged letters.

"The demo," a voice said. "We have a few questions about that."

"What kind of questions?" Wassermann asked.

"Serious questions. For instance, we were wondering about this pallet shift we're getting. We called your tech support people about that. And the directory logic. Those are two of our major concerns." I noticed then that Barnes was crying, a slight wetness around the eyes that I would have passed off as a cold or allergies if not for the quiver in his lip. "We were also wondering about importing files. There seems to be a serious bug in the methodology there."

"Bug?" Barnes said. "That's a feature."

"It looks like a bug to me," one of them finally said after a long pause. The delicate balance was shuddering, threatening to break.

Barnes half stood, as if he wanted to head off somewhere

but wasn't sure where, and leaned toward the speaker. "You're using the software incorrectly. We've gone over this before."

"We have talked about this. A number of times," the first voice said. "That's why it's so upsetting."

"It is upsetting," Barnes said. Agreement of a sort. Then another soft pause. Then nothing. They had hung up the phone.

Barnes was standing, staring at the wall, motionless. Wassermann had his head back and eyes closed, as if listening intently to the single note of the dial tone. I imagined someone gently scrolling through the network directory and noticing unfamiliar names that should have been deleted, people fired long ago. Small markers in two columns, names and dates. Cemetery neatness. I thought of a person moving through the voice mail system, punching ones and twos, rooting deeper and deeper, from stem to stem, and finding ghost messages from people who no longer existed here except as dim images in the company brain. My happy voice saying, *please leave a message and I'll get back to you.*

"I have to be somewhere," I said.

The department secretary wasn't at her desk and neither was her sweater, which she always kept on the back of her chair in case the air-conditioning got too cold.

I found a Post-it note stuck to my terminal saying that the vice president of something wanted to see me. I didn't recognize the handwriting. A cartoon in the upper left-hand corner showed a fat orange cat sleeping in a hammock, an image that seemed completely incongruous. The more I looked at it the more sinister it became, and I had to force myself to put it down. I fished my socks out of the wastebasket, put one in each pocket, and headed toward my destiny.

I bumped into Natalie in the hall. She was holding a copy-paper box packed with odds and ends: papers and folders, a framed photograph of her cocker spaniel, a baseball she would toss from hand to hand when having a bad day. "Walk with me," I said without stopping, and she moved up alongside.

"Did you hear?" she asked.

"I heard," I said.

"Where are you going?"

"This way," I said. "I'm going this way."

"What?" she said. "Where?"

"Outside. Then to my car. After that I'm not sure. Maybe far away. Far away would be good." I had reached the elevator. A young boy held the door for me, a bike messenger dressed in ripped jeans and retro-chic wraparound sunglasses. "Come with me," I said to her. She looked at her box of things. I thought of the empty closets in my house, the unread newspapers, the bed that seemed to grow wider the more I looked at it, the vast spaces to fill.

"You know I can't," she said.

The kid smirked and sniffed and looked as bored as a person could look. "Fine," I said and stepped into the elevator. The kid had already punched up the ground floor, and the doors closed behind me. I turned to him, pointed at his sunglasses. "I'll give you fifty dollars for those."

When I got outside I broke into a run across the parking lot toward my Explorer, clicking off the alarm as I went. I slid the air-conditioning to full, gunned the engine for effect, and moved past the guard post, going twice the speed limit as soon as I passed the yellow-painted speed bump. I glanced to my left when I reached the stop sign at the exit of the industrial park, accelerating into the turn with the kind of relaxed intuition that comes from doing something again and again. As soon as I rounded the corner I slipped the car into fourth, then fifth, letting my hand linger on the stick shift, feeling the vibration of the engine that seemed to be focused there. I sped up more, just to experience the change of sensation against my palm.

In five minutes I had reached the main road, which was clogged with four o'clock commuters getting a head start for home. A few cars were turning around on the highway on-ramp, driving up over the curb and across the neat grass strip that separated the two roads. I tapped the dash with both hands, keeping awkward time to the song on the radio as we lurched forward, merging with the main flow. There was something almost biological in the way the cars clung together, bumpers almost touching bumpers, like blood cells pumping through an artery. The radio played a dance song, slinky sweet, turned so low I could hear only muffled drums and some semblance of a voice.

The traffic picked up speed past a truck with emergency flashers on. I imagined the insides of each vehicle, thousands of synchronized parts sparking and clicking: a seemingly simple thing turned frighteningly complex. I cranked the radio louder, punched up an all-news station. I reclined my seat, leaning my head back so that I felt as if I were sitting dreamily in a dentist's chair, letting some drug work itself through me. There was a busy, antlike desperation in the way the cars tried to narrow the space in front of them. People leaned on their horns if someone else grew lax and let the car in front gain too much distance. We all have to work together here, seemed to be the consensus, like it or not.

"It's a real battle out there this afternoon," the traffic reporter was saying. "It's congested. It's constipated. It's complete entropy." I looked to my left out the window, and I could see a helicopter circling in the distance. I wondered if the man on the radio and the man in the helicopter were the same. My foot moved to the brake, and I heard a sharp honk from behind me, then a second, longer this time. I slapped my horn twice in reply and then held it down until the car to my right leaned on his. Two more horns behind bleated out together, then another one ahead—sporadic bovine noise, instinctive call and response. When I closed my eyes I pictured the line of cars as a procession of clumsy animals, starved and lost, migrating blind to an unknown destination. "Bumper to bumper," the reporter was saying.

I dropped my car into park and set the brake, then opened my door and stepped out into the breakdown lane, into the shiny bits of glass, as fine and delicate as broken shells on the beach, and the sand and litter and shredded tire rubber. The person in the car in front of mine turned her head and stared. I didn't stare back. I was taking off my jacket. I was taking off my tie. I was straddling the guardrail, and then I was scrambling down the embankment. In passing I remembered that my car engine was running, that the door was wide open like a crippled bird with only one wing. More horns were beginning to sound from further away, until we were all joined by that beautiful, aching music.

The stones chaffed my feet as I walked, and I wondered if the woods were surrounded by highway like a small island. The trees were getting thicker and I had to duck under branches. A wet leaf the shape of an arrowhead was stuck to my bare chest. I was cold and warm at the same time. Except for my boxers, I was now as naked as an elk. Then they were off too. I clutched them in my hand and then dropped them to the ground, leaving a trail behind me for other lost souls to follow when they went over the edge.

Justin was in love with a girl whose brother had been disfig-
ured by fire. The kids called him Barbecue, but only behind
his back, because he stood over six feet tall, with thick biceps,
a stomach hard from a regimen of sit-ups, and crossed dag-
gers tattooed on his throat just below the scars. The face itself
was a sort of tattoo as well—the smudged gray red of the skin
around the cheeks, the even furrows across the forehead. The
symmetry of the burns seemed artful, almost intentional. His
sunken left eye was sealed closed, something white collected
around the slit.

His real name was Steven Adams, and his sister's name was
Gerri, and Justin didn't just love her, he ached for her. Her
parents were away in Europe for the summer, and Justin had
taken to staying with her often in her room. As they groped
each other on her neatly made bed, he listened to the brother
down deep in the house lifting weights—the clatter of the

metal, the occasional grunting yell, and a faint rasping sound that may have been the air conditioner but Justin imagined as heavy breathing. It sounded a lot like their own breath—quick, desperate, and frustrated.

"Can you hear him?" Justin asked, throwing his legs over the side of the bed.

"Yeah," Gerri said. "He's angry."

"Yeah," he said, and he hunched there, his forearms across his knees, looking at her wall.

It was late June. Her parents would return in August, and Gerri's room would become as remote to him then as Europe was now. Listening to Barbecue and thinking about places he had never been, Justin became remote himself. "Nothing," he said when Gerri asked him what he was thinking. She put her hand on his bare back, and as she rubbed circles on his body, he felt something dark well up inside him—a self-disgust that made him want to slither out of his own skin. He tried to push it down by force of will.

"Are you sure?" she asked. This time he didn't bother answering. He turned to her, hand on her shoulder, lips against her neck.

"No," she said.

He had never given her an orgasm, never traveled anywhere distant with her, never revealed the worst parts of himself to her, never had his affection tested by crisis. He had never told her just how much he loved her, although he had said he loved her—but those two things seemed far apart at that moment in the dimness of her room. "I love you," he said forcefully but quietly, and he waited for the sadness that came into her eyes whenever he said these words.

Her hand was still on his back, but she was silent, and so

he took hold of her arm and pushed her back on the bed. He didn't want tenderness from her—that was too close to pity. He could feel the blood pumping in her wrist. In his mind he was already looking past this to the time when she would be asleep while he was still awake, and then the next morning when he would run across town, first one mile, then three, then six and eight and nine. He was running ten miles a day lately.

"Stop," she said, so he stood without looking at her. It had been an empty gesture anyway. He wasn't even hard.

He left the room still not looking at her, sliding his fingers along the wall as he walked toward the lit room at the end of the upstairs corridor. In the bathroom he dropped his pants and listened to the water in the bowl. On the floor to one side of the toilet there were women's magazines and catalogs filled with oak furniture and cashmere sweaters. There were also a couple of recent postcards, one from Switzerland and one from Ireland.

Justin couldn't stop thinking about fire. It was what he thought about when he had twisted with Gerri on her bed, and it was what he thought about as the sound of water in the bowl quieted to a trickle and he held himself. He closed his eyes and wondered what it must have felt like for Barbecue—for Steve. If a person, an average person, were to tabulate his pain—all the cuts, scrapes, broken bones, and heartbreaks—would they add up to that one event?

Imagining that pain reminded him of his own—the sharp particulars of that one day in the woods. That memory was his. He possessed it the way Gerri's family possessed their house, and he entered into it with the same mix of trepidation and happiness: the walk by the hospital into the trees, emerging through the bushes and then kneeling by the shallow pond, the old shed across the water surrounded by rusted barbed wire and broken liquor bottles. And then they were coming out of the woods, and then his hand was slippery and he felt the shame, suddenly but with such familiarity that it was a seamless part of the pleasure. As he slid his thumb and finger down his cock he imagined Gerri opening the bathroom door, and that added to both the shame and the satisfaction—bound them together in a tight knot.

If she came in, he thought, then he would have to explain.

He found the washcloth he normally used on the bottom shelf of the cabinet, wet it, and rubbed it over his belly and privates. The cloth was cold—he hadn't let the water run long enough—but he didn't care. In the early stages of a jog, before he was in his rhythm, he often felt like his body was something separate from who he was—something that contained him but wasn't him. He felt that way as he pushed the cloth over his stomach, absorbed in the give of his muscles and skin. Semen had collected in his belly button. He cleaned it roughly with his finger, then wiped his hands and tugged up his jeans.

He didn't want to return to Gerri's bedroom, so he headed downstairs, where he killed time examining objects on the fireplace mantel—small oriental figurines with sly grins, intricately carved nonsense art, metal-framed photographs of Gerri's parents smiling in some desert climate. Bored, he crossed the room in the near dark and sat at the piano. He spun around one revolution on the oak stool, then raised his hands as if to bring them down with a clamor.

The first week Gerri's parents were away he slept in the guest room and upon waking in the morning he heard the piano and what he thought was the clatter of pots and pans from the kitchen. Sometimes in his drowsiness he assumed it was his mother, but then he remembered that he was in someone else's house and that the sound of the piano was Gerri practicing and the metallic clatter was Barbecue in the garage working on the Plymouth Road Runner—or maybe the Mercedes if he was feeling more generous. Justin felt a part of the rhythm of their house then, even if it was only till his feet hit the floor. He was always late for work and had to dress in a rush and push himself on the run there, up the long, slow hill that led to Main Street.

When he arrived at the service station and took a shower in the narrow stall out back, he would hold that memory of waking as the trickle of water came down into his cupped hands. He shook his hair dry, changed into his work clothes, and then he tried to hold onto it as he worked, in the way he held onto the melody Gerri had been practicing. He let it move through his head while he pumped gas and made change and stacked cases of oil, and it was enough to make him feel like an imposter in his day, because when customers glanced out their car windows and said, "Fill it up," they were speaking to someone in disguise. They didn't know where he had come from that morning, where he would return that night, didn't know his history. His face didn't even register to them, just his general shape—a dirty hand taking their credit cards.

You should just tell her, he sometimes thought in a moment of recklessness when they were speaking kindly to each other. But he couldn't. On her bureau Gerri had small ceramic statues of horses and rabbits and dragons that Justin had never touched. It hurt just to look at them. Her sweaters smelled of something sweet like baby powder, and they came in colors like *persimmon* and *peacock* and *charcoal heather.* "You look so collegiate today," he sneered at her when they weren't getting along, which seemed to be more and more as the summer inched forward.

Justin stood up from the piano stool, gave it another spin, and ran his fingers along the black keys lightly enough that they did not play. He tried to guess what it cost, and when he realized he had no idea, he stepped away from it into the next room.

The kitchen smelled of the strawberry candles Gerri was always lighting and placing precariously around the house. His own house smelled of his mother's cooking—pork chops, haddock, corned beef and cabbage—and her cigarettes, which she smoked standing in the doorway between the kitchen and living room so she could watch television while she cooked. Wicker baskets and strings of garlic hung from the beams above his head. The high ceilings in Gerri's house made Justin feel small—the way he also felt in relation to Gerri herself, he realized. She was lovely in a way that could make him feel diminished. Almost homely. "You're gorgeous," she told him once when kissing his chest, and it seemed like he had been chosen, the way he had been chosen at other times in his life—chosen to work for Sanborn's Automotive, a good, easy job he tried hard to dislike; chosen to be the son of a single parent; chosen that time in the woods near the hospital when he was ten.

The microwave clock showed it was past midnight. He felt like an intruder, and when he tried the fantasy on for size—when he imagined himself creeping through the house, rifling through drawers, stealing the mother's necklaces and rings—he was surprised to find that it fit relatively comfortably. Then he imagined Gerri catching him, and in the fantasy she knew him even though he was somebody else. She touched him and called him by name, and once again he was ashamed and pleased.

He switched on a light over the stove and grabbed himself a glass, feeling less like an intruder now and more like what he was—a visitor. As he poured himself some water he looked at his reflection in the window above the sink. He had never liked his nose. He didn't like his eyes either, he decided, although Gerri had said they were his best feature. He still didn't like his chest, almost hairless except for strands of blond and flecked with small red dots. He lifted the glass to his lips and drank it down, looking past his reflection at the yard.

That's when he noticed Barbecue standing on the porch smoking a cigarette and looking at the yard just as Justin had been doing. He was dressed in a white V-neck T-shirt and was smiling out one side of his mouth as he took a long drag. He held a Beck's bottle in his other hand, into which he tapped the end of the cigarette. Their eyes met. At first Justin didn't think Barbecue had noticed him, but then he made a short poking gesture with the bottle, calling him outside.

There were so many rumors about Barbecue that he seemed to be made of stories, like someone who has been dead for years existing only as photographs and words. There was the story about Providence, Rhode Island. Supposedly he drove down there every weekend and blew money on drugs and prostitutes. There was the story that his father—Gerri's father—hit him. Kids had seen bruises. But just one look at Barbecue—the knots of muscles in his arms and neck—and it was hard to believe that he wouldn't fight back. And if he fought back, wouldn't he win? His father was a thin man, short, with a hunched, nervous manner. A financial analyst in Boston.

Barbecue's face had been burned for as long as Justin could remember. Justin wasn't sure of the cause, although again there were rumors—a grease fire, an explosion in the garage, a lawn mower accident of all things. To Justin it simply seemed like Barbecue had come back damaged from a war nobody else had even known about. He set down the glass and headed out to the porch.

"Hey, hey," Barbecue said. "Welcome, fellow insomniac."

"Hello, Steve," Justin said without looking at him. He looked at the yard instead. They were both staring at the same dark spot as if something dangerous were prowling out there.

Barbecue snickered. "So," he said. "So, so, so." When he talked, his mouth moved from side to side as if he was gnawing something sinewy. "You like my sister," he said.

"Very much," Justin said.

"Very much," Barbecue repeated back to him as if it was something funny. He had Gerri's eyes, sort of. One of them anyway. The good right one looked like Gerri's, large and dark. "So," he pit-patted again. "So, so, so." Justin noticed then that Barbecue had rolled his cigarette himself. Barbecue inhaled deeply, blew sweet smelling smoke toward the yard, and said, "Are your intentions honorable? Isn't that what I'm supposed to ask? Are your intentions honorable?"

Justin didn't say anything.

"I'm just kidding you, man," Barbecue said.

"I know."

"But are they? Are they honorable?"

"I'm crazy about her, if that's what you mean," Justin said.

"Crazy for her, huh? Good for you. That's great. Star-crossed lovers. I can get behind that. I'll throw my support your way. My father, on the other hand, he's a different story." He took another long toke and continued. "She's going to Harvard or Yale or somewhere like that. Where are you going? That's the big question, I guess. But I'm with you, man. I'm on your side.

I sympathize with the disenfranchised." He looked away from the yard and at Justin now. "You try awful hard, don't you?"

Another silence. Then Justin said, "What do you mean?"

"I can hear you guys up there. I may look like Frankenstein, but I'm not as dumb as him, you know. I can put two and two together."

Justin wanted a drag on that cigarette. It would calm him down, smooth him out. Maybe somehow it would bring them closer together. He wanted to talk, but not like this.

"I'm just kidding again, relax," Barbecue said. "Just chalk it up to bitterness. I'll give you three guesses why I'm bitter. You want to guess?"

"No," Justin said. "That's okay."

"Okay, sure," Barbecue said and looked back at the yard.

Justin studied his face, and the more he looked at it, the more he wanted to look. In the dark, the lines gouged in Barbecue's cheeks seemed as much from age as violence. He decided he could learn a lot from someone with a face like that. "How old were you when it happened?" Justin asked.

"When what happened?" Eyes on the yard. Deadpan.

"You know."

"My virginity? Sixteen. A year younger than my sister." A small pause. A bent smirk. A short drag. "But that's not what you mean. You mean the face. That's what you mean. And the funny thing, it's not even the worst part. The worst is down here where you can't see it." He slid his open hand over his chest and belly. "Anyway, that happened when I was twelve. Gerri doesn't talk about me, huh? I'm hurt." Another drag. Then he held out the shrunken roach to Justin, who took it. "There you go," Barbecue said.

Justin blew smoke from his nose and mouth and passed back

the joint. He had never done this sort of thing with Gerri, and he guessed she wouldn't approve of his doing it with someone else, especially her brother, whom she spoke to only when asking for something like phone messages. He had seen how they orbited around each other.

Justin tried not to stare. He stared anyway. A person with a face like that would understand.

Barbecue wet his fingers on his tongue, snuffed the joint, and said, "I think it's time for bed. Dream some nice dreams. Whisper sweet nothings in her ear or something."

Justin guessed that Barbecue hated and loved his sister fiercely in some gnarled combination of feeling. Justin could understand that. It was like he was seeing himself for the first time, he decided, as if Barbecue were a mirror. Some small part of himself—the worst part, he noted—hated her too, for being so pristine, so smart, for sleeping peacefully upstairs while he was awake, for the look in her eyes. He hated her for not giving him what he wanted, although he didn't know what that was exactly, and he hated himself for hating her, and what the hell was he doing out here anyway, smoking marijuana with her older brother? He took a deep breath and said, "Good night. Maybe I'll see you in the morning."

Justin waited until he heard Barbecue's feet on the stairs, then headed into the garage. The chrome on the Road Runner had been polished until it glistened. The hood was open, and when Justin bent down over the engine he saw that it was as clean as the outside. He reached in and touched the engine block and thought again of being caught, turning to see Barbecue in the doorway, but he heard no sound except his own footsteps on the cement as he walked around to the rear bumper.

Tools and spray cans littered the concrete floor. Barbecue

had been grinding out a small rust spot on the fender. Justin knelt and rubbed the spot with sandpaper folded into a hard square. It wouldn't be that difficult, he decided, to get to know him.

The first time Justin had met Gerri she had surprised him. She had pointed at him and said, "You're that guy who runs around town. I've seen you in thunderstorms," and he had been startled to hear her voice addressing him. Then she had smiled and closed her hand into a fist and put it to her chin. He had come into the library to get a drink from the water fountain, and as he passed her she looked up from her books as if she had been waiting for him.

There had been stick drawings of animals in the margins of her notebook.

He had known her too, through the stories about her brother, and because her father was well known in town. He had even known her name and that she attended the private school in Exeter. He had known she played piano. When there was talk about Barbecue, it usually got around to her piano playing, which was supposed to be world class, according to one of Justin's coworkers at the station. There was even talk about her going to a conservatory, which he found out later was not true. She was not as good as people thought. "It's a way to keep me occupied," she said once with a laugh. "My parents are always trying to find ways to keep me *occupied*."

"He has an in-ground pool," Justin had told his mother the first time he mentioned that he was spending the night at his friend's house.

His mother was one of the few people in town who had avoided getting to know Barbecue by reputation, and she seemed happy to hear Justin had a close friend, maybe happy enough not to worry about not seeing him lately. "You spend too much time locked up by yourself in your room," she had told him more than once. "Or running. I read somewhere that it's not as healthy a sport as people might think. And there are the cars."

"Sure," he would answer as he headed to the bathroom. It was good to be away from there—he was especially sure of it whenever he got back. There was a sound she made when she sat down, a defeated sigh, and a strained groan when she stood up, and a small mirror in the bathroom with water stains across it that he had to look into whenever he brushed his teeth. There were old photos of himself in the living room, his hair wet from swimming. Looking at them, he wished they didn't exist.

"How is Steven?" she sometimes asked over dinner, and he wondered if she knew. If she did, he was sure she wouldn't say. That's how it worked between them. They had reached that agreement long ago.

"Pretty good," he said, and it wasn't really a lie, although it had started out as one, because as the summer progressed, as the postcards and packages arrived from different European cities, Justin and Barbecue talked more. The garage was cool and dark, and while Barbecue worked on his car late into the night, Justin sat against the brick wall, and Barbecue sometimes opened his hand and asked for a tool or the small rainbow-painted pipe with the blackened screen in its bowl. Eventually Justin began packing it himself and taking a toke when he first made an appearance, blowing the smoke out through his nose and closing his eyes.

"The Superbird. Now that was a car," Barbecue said once as he looked down into the engine skeptically. "Nineteen seventy was a great year for cars. It was all downhill after emissions testing."

"Sure," Justin replied.

"Not that I'm complaining. Nineteen seventy-four was a good year too. The last one. Pass me that rag."

The pool filter was humming out in the yard. Justin closed his eyes and listened to it, listened to Barbecue saying, "People think I am the way I am because of the accident. They think it's simple. But it's not. Ah, well. It gives me an excuse, I guess. It's worth something, or at least it was, once upon a time. When I was younger I was the little scarred angel. The accident was the reason for every bad thing I did. I'd steal a cookie. It was the accident. I'd shoot a pigeon with a BB gun. The accident. But there's only so much mileage you can get out of that. So what, though, right? I don't mind being the boogeyman. Take a look at this for me. It's all fucked up."

Gerri was upstairs during all of this, sleeping or mulling over one of their arguments. Justin and Barbecue never talked about her—they talked about the cracked carburetor in the Mercedes, the long stretch of hot weather, the ticking down of the summer days—but she was a presence nonetheless. One of the cars he was working on was for her, after all.

It had taken Justin a while to figure that out. There were two cars in the garage, two outside, one for each member of the family. Barbecue drove the Plymouth and the Explorer, which sometimes came home with long splatters of mud along the sides. Justin and Gerri did not drive often, but the first time they did—to a movie showing at the small one-screen theater in town—they took the Explorer. "She left the seat forward," Barbecue said the next night. "I hate when she does that."

"Yeah," Justin said, although it had been he who had driven.

"It'll be good when I get this done," he said, and he gave the Mercedes a tap on the fender, as if for luck. "That way she won't be messing with my shit anymore. She's going to love it too. She better love it anyway, right?"

"Right," Justin said. He pictured her stopped at a traffic light in Boston, two years older, head turned so she could look at the Charles River and the faces of the pedestrians coming toward her in the crosswalk — a collage of faces, some of them interesting. She would be thinking about her classes, the summer after this one, the rest of her life.

"I think the heat guard is loose," Justin told him.

"I know," Barbecue said. "Take a look at the manifold for me. Make yourself useful."

It was weeks later when Justin would finally tell him the story that balanced them — the story that explained. "I was ten years old," he would say, remembering that Barbecue had been twelve.

It was deep in the summer when Gerri said to him, "What's the matter? Don't you find me attractive?" She was straddling him, her hands on his chest, and her voice had the steady tone of someone who was more bored than annoyed. He gently pushed her off, stood up, and found his jeans on the floor. She watched from the bed as he slipped his foot into one pant leg, then the other, and pulled them on. When he made a move to leave, to walk down the hall to the bathroom and shut the door, she said, "Wait, Justin. Don't do that."

"Do what?" he said, as he tugged up his zipper.

"You *know* what," she said, and he heard anger in her voice, a coldness that reminded him of her brother.

"I don't know," he said, because that was all he could think to say. Although his fingers were working the buttons of his shirt, he still felt naked. She was staring him down from the bed as if the door was already open and he was huddled at the far end of the darkened hall. He imagined holding himself—eyes closed, wrist jerking—under that stare, and he grew flushed and hard, tight against his jeans. He wondered if she noticed.

"You know what," she said, "and so do I."

They were delivering the lines they had written in their heads all summer. He tried out another one just to see the expression on her face. "What do you know about anything?" he said. "Spoiled rich girl." He gave the knickknacks on her bureau as dark a look as he could and then opened the door.

He had taken a few steps down the hall when Gerri grabbed up one of her jewelry boxes and threw it after him. It struck the wall behind his head, not hard enough to break but hard enough that it popped open and sent earrings and necklaces to the carpet. He bent down to gather them up in both hands.

"Get away from that. Those are mine," she said. She stood over him, and he felt as small as he had ever felt in this house.

"Listen," he said. "I'm sorry."

She reached out to touch the top of his head. He thought of sliding up her body, kissing her mouth, pressing up against her and letting her discover how much he wanted her. Which is what he did. He wasn't quite aware that he was doing it. She put both hands against his chest and pushed him back. "Get out, Justin," she said. "Get out of my house." Those words, *my house*, were like another push, so he pushed her back. Her foot hit the jewelry box, and it made a small cracking sound. She glanced down at it and then at him—that same level stare—and he almost said he was sorry again. She stepped toward him, arms up, and then she was stepping backward again, her hand

THE UGLIEST BOY 203

holding her cheek, and he was heading down the hall, saying, "I'm going now. I'm going."

Barbecue was in the garage polishing his car with Windex and a soft cloth. Justin walked in, rested his back against the cool wall, and watched him work. He would spray the hubcap, rub circles in it, stare at it, and then start over. After a while Justin slid down into a crouching position.

"I don't know what she sees in me," he said, surprised at his own words, and Barbecue's too when he replied, "That's easy. You're handsome." His face pulled into a gnarled smile, and Justin wondered if he had heard them upstairs a few minutes before. He had probably been sitting at the same wheel, shining the same hubcap, when Gerri had been throwing her jewelry box.

"It looks good," Justin told him, and they both scrutinized the hubcap.

"Thanks," he said. "I aim to please." He stood up and rubbed his hands on his thighs. "Do you want to go for a drive?" Justin said yes too quickly, and Barbecue's face ticked again. "Then you should probably buy a car one of these days, shouldn't you? Instead of running all around town, you could do what I do."

He thought of driving with his mother, the seat belts across their chests, the craning of her neck and the slow roll through the intersection—that feeling that something awful might happen any second.

"You're all fidgety tonight," Barbecue said. "More than usual."

"Yeah," Justin said, and at that moment he wanted an end to secrets. He wanted to see shock in Barbecue's face, buried in the gashes and bruised scars. He thought of the woods near the hospital, the pond and its fishy smell. Sometimes it was like it had never happened. Other times it was like yesterday—like it had been only hours since they told him that his skin was like cream.

"What time is it?" Barbecue asked him.

"I don't know."

"I guess you should probably head home, huh?"

"Yeah," Justin said, and he thought of Gerri reaching for her cheek as he turned and headed to the stairs. By the time he had reached the landing she would have been kneeling to pick up her jewelry. In his mind's eye he could see her still naked, three or four elegant necklaces looped around her palm. He wondered if the box had broken, if she had been crying, if she was crying now as he walked into the cool night air. Not knowing seemed a worse crime than the slap itself. The punch, he corrected, trying to find the right name for what had happened, the right place for it in his head. He couldn't remember if his fingers had been closed or open or the sound it made when he struck her.

The garage lights clicked off behind him, and he stepped down the walkway and around the side of the house in darkness.

"Ich wünschte du wärst hier," the postcard said. Three newspapers rolled into tight batons stuck up from the mailbox along with the postcard, junk mail, and a credit card bill for the meals Gerri's parents were eating in small Parisian cafes. Nobody had taken in the mail since Justin had been there two days before. During the past month, it had become his job. He slipped the postcard back into the mailbox, climbed the front stairs, and rang the bell.

When nobody came to the door, he took some of the small

stones from around the shrubs, stones as white and smooth as teeth, and threw them at Gerri's window. The shades remained drawn. He thought about yelling up for her—or maybe stealing the mail and leaving. Anything seemed possible. It was raining lightly and his T-shirt was so wet that he could see through it. He had saved the largest rock for last. He threw it overhand, hard, and it hit the gutter with a bang. Nothing. He thought of Gerri sitting on the edge of her bed, a bruise on her cheek. He placed the bruise there carefully with his imagination as a way to punish himself. The slap had probably not been hard enough to cause it—his hand had been open, he was practically sure of it—but he wanted to make entirely sure. If he could see her, he could talk to her, and he could explain.

When he headed around the back of the house, Barbecue seemed to be waiting for him. "How are you doing?" he asked, and Justin thought that maybe this was the meeting he had actually come for.

"Fine," he said as he climbed the stairs to the patio. He looked up at the shaded windows.

"Why don't you give Gerri a little breather, okay?" Barbecue said. "You're upset and she's upset."

He wasn't upset, although being told he was upset made him upset. He said, "I just need to talk to her for a minute."

"Sorry," Barbecue said. He sounded like he meant it.

"A minute," Justin said.

"No," Barbecue said.

"No," Justin repeated, trying the word out.

"That's right."

He didn't really know what he wanted to do, except that he wanted to get into the house. He would figure everything else out after that. He ducked his head and stepped forward. Barbecue put his hand on his shoulder. It was the first time they had touched.

Justin turned and was going to say something when he realized that he was sitting on the grass. He opened his eyes and saw flecks of red on his T-shirt and expected a second punch, but nothing came. His hands were warm and wet and bloody, as if he had been the one hitting someone. Which he had been, he realized, just two days before. He felt some satisfaction from having the roles reversed. Maybe Barbecue did too.

Blood was running from his nose into his palms, but he didn't feel pain. He was more aware of the salty taste of the blood and the weakness in his legs, as if he had been running straight out. In a way Barbecue had saved him from embarrassment. If he had gone into the house, what would he have done, what would he have said?

He coughed and then vomited with a sharp hacking sound. A trail of spittle dangled from his mouth. He closed his eyes again and heard Barbecue say, "Oh, man."

They both looked down at what he had done. Then Justin heard himself say, "I'm sorry." He coughed again and wiped his face with the back of his hand.

A noise came from the house. Gerri was practicing. He could hear the piano faintly from the porch, and he understood better than ever why people might think she was going to Julliard or somewhere. Distance gave it false poignancy—delicate music almost not there at all. And there was the house—windows with fake black shutters that didn't really close, the door with its circular stained glass window, the piano hidden somewhere inside, and the player hidden too, her long blonde hair tied back, her body at attention. Of course she would have sounded beautiful, to the mailman, say, delivering a postcard from Portugal.

"Don't try to stand," Barbecue said. "Give yourself a minute."

"Okay," Justin said, but he struggled to get to his feet. He knew what he had to do.

This would be the way to tell Gerri. Give the story to her brother and let him pass it along to her. He staggered up and coughed again. "I have something to tell you," he said.

"What is it?" Barbecue asked.

"Well," Justin said, "it's complicated," and stepped back onto the patio.

Barbecue laughed. "It always is."

"That's true," Justin said. "That's true." And he took a step down, then another, until he was standing on the grass again. He started to talk. Then he told him. "I was ten years old," he said.

It had happened out behind the playground near dusk, when the pool was closed and most of the kids had already gone home in groups of two or three. The playground didn't exist anymore, or the woods behind it, but back then you could walk a rocky trail that led to a pond where kids sometimes caught frogs. That's what Justin was doing—looking for frogs. He must have figured it was a good time to look for them. The streetlights were on. It was quiet.

"There were two of them," he told Barbecue. He remembered this part vividly—kneeling down, the plastic toes of his high-top sneakers spattered with pond mud, then looking up and seeing the two men. He remembered two of them, although sometimes their faces were the same face, one face shared between the two. One of them made a guttural sound like *excuse me*, like *what are you doing here?* Or maybe it was one of the frogs.

They said something to him, something friendly, something

coaxing. One was standing slightly in front of the other, and for a second Justin thought they were carrying something like a heavy log or stick, but they weren't. It was just the way the shadows were falling. Maybe they were and they dropped it as soon as they saw him. The grass was tall, up to his knees. "My feet were covered with mud," he said.

He remembered this much—one was fat, one was skinny, gawky almost. They both wore baseball caps. What did they say? It was hard to remember, hard to see them even, in that dusky light, like shining a flashlight down a well. They separated, one stepping clockwise around the pond, one counterclockwise. Although they didn't separate so much as blur, like the lens of his memory was moving out of focus. It was confusing trying to remember exactly what had happened.

Sometimes they wore the same face.

"I didn't move an inch," Justin said. The nearest house was half a mile away. A family was eating dinner there, or watching television. He remembered walking past once and seeing the blue screen through the window.

Something was almost comforting about the way they held him, one around the shoulders, one around the waist, and pushed him down. The mud was warm and smelled of tadpoles, but cooler beneath the surface, like something half cooked. He made his hand into a fist and felt the coolness squeeze through his fingers. He bit down on something. His tongue. They were talking to him quietly, repeating each other's words. There was a weight, a pressure, on his shoulders and the small of his back. Was there pain? There must have been pain.

They were pulling down his jeans, tugging at his shirt. They hushed him the way the doctor hushed him, reassured him, told him it was okay, and he felt like he had to believe them.

Not less than a hundred yards away kids were playing on swing sets, tossing basketballs, seeing how much time they could squeeze out of the day before heading home to supper. Which wasn't right. There was no one else around. But still he swore he heard something. "I thought I heard kids laughing," he told him, "and then I remember worrying about dinner."

He was going to be late. But maybe not. They were quick about it. They were efficient. They told him not to worry and not to tell anyone. He remembered them telling him please. Please don't tell anyone. There was shame in their voices, although maybe not, because that seemed unlikely, and maybe it was just one voice. The voice told him that he was pretty and talked about his body parts. Broke him down, subdivided him. Nice lips. Nice legs. Nice ass. He didn't know how he'd ever put himself back together again. He clenched at the mud and hoped they wouldn't take his money, because he had five dollars in his wallet.

Justin didn't tell Barbecue everything, of course. He didn't talk about how strong he felt afterward, walking home, because that seemed absurd. Why would he feel strong? But he did. He did tell him, though, how he threw away his shirt, his underwear, his jeans, his socks even. He put it all in one of the trash bags of leaves he had raked that weekend to earn the five dollars they hadn't taken. He put the bag out behind the shed on the outskirts of the property. A neighborhood dog was with him when he did it, circling around his feet.

"Two of them?" Barbecue asked. Something about that did seem insane, impossible. Justin could see Barbecue's confusion somewhere in the gnarled expression as he tried to grasp it, measure it against his own pain.

Justin shrugged and moved to go. His nose was still bleeding, and now it was starting to hurt. He said, "I just wanted to talk to her."

"She doesn't want to see you anymore, you know," Barbecue said. "She's been thinking about it for a long time, but she hasn't had the heart. She waited too long. That's what I told her. Way too long. But she felt sorry for you. And she was hoping."

"She was hoping," Justin said.

"That's right," he said. "She was hoping."

Justin turned and looked back at the yard, then up at the windows on the second floor of the house.

"She has a lot of hope," Barbecue said, and after thinking for a second, "She's full of hope." The way he said it sounded almost paternal but also bitter, as if he had said, she's full of it, full of shit. Despite himself Justin felt almost insulted on Gerri's behalf. It was Barbecue's smile that did it. Justin didn't like it when he smiled like that.

"Well, tell her," Justin said. He felt a lump in his throat. He put a foot on the first step again, his hand on the railing. "You know, tell her."

"I'm not going to do that."

"Why?"

"You know why."

Justin stood there looking up into Barbecue's face. He felt like he could stand there forever and that Barbecue could stand there forever too, looking deeply into each other. The piano was playing from inside the house.

On the way home he crossed through downtown, past the library with its rickety clock tower, past the bank signs blinking the time and temperature, walking on the side of the road against a steady flow of headlights. Sometimes he noticed the face of a driver watching him as the car slipped past. They must have wondered where he was going and what had happened to him. He had not bothered to clean his face or his shirt. He could feel the blood around his nostrils. The rain was warm and he was strangely happy.

He crossed against the light, past a middle-aged woman looking at him from inside her Civic. He was a mystery to her, he decided, and the thought made him feel tougher in his isolation. He was a story they were going to tell over her dinner table that night, but not the *right* story. He jumped to the curb and jogged down the sidewalk into an alley.

When he arrived home he went inside and thought briefly about heading to the bathroom so that his mother would not see his face, but instead he stood there on her braided throw rug and waited for her to come in. She was probably upstairs in bed, awake, listening to talk radio. Then he could hear her moving around—her steps soft as if she did not want to be heard.

She did not gasp or even look very shocked when she saw him. Her hands didn't rise to her mouth in surprise. She didn't yell. She said, "What did he do to you?" and anger was in her voice. She knew who had done it. That much was easy to figure out.

"It was just a little fight," he said. She was rubbing a warm cloth down his face. He hadn't even realized she had gone to get it until he felt it against his skin. "Don't," he said. "That hurts."

When he ran through the city that September, nose swollen, both eyes black and yellow like a mask, people waved and yelled out to him. They wanted to talk to him, because the break had been so bad, because the family had been rich and they had given Justin's family—Justin's mother—more than a little money, and because the punch had been thrown by one of the toughest kids in town. The daughter, the one who played the piano, she was at Princeton now, wasn't she?

Justin stopped and as he stretched his calves, they asked how he was doing, and if he could breathe okay, running the way he was with his nose busted up like that. He straightened up and motioned north and talked about the house where he had spent his summer. It was like he had just returned from a far-away country and he was talking about his trip. The story he told them grew shorter as he learned how to tell it, one variation for the concerned mothers, a different one for the girls his age, another for the joking middle-aged men. "But you should see the other guy, right?" one of them said, and then he slapped his shoulder and smiled as if they were friends.

Sometimes Justin saw the Road Runner parked around town, straddling two spaces at the edge of a parking lot, and he thought about lingering there—leaning on the warm hood—but he never did, and he didn't see it often, and then not at all.

Sometimes I wake in the middle of the night. Maybe it's some nocturnal animal scrambling along the gutter or an error in my body clock or the way my husband moves next to me, but something opens my eyes. There's a clock radio on my side of the bed, and one on the other side too, set ten minutes fast so that Nicholas won't be late for work in the mornings. I turn my head and note the time: midnight, one o'clock, two-thirty. Then I pull the sheets back. Nicholas is sleeping soundly. He is already past this moment, out ahead of me by ten minutes.

We live in an open-concept house designed by a trendy Connecticut architectural firm. The theory behind their designs is this: leave the occupants no place to hide. If I were to turn left as I walked down the hall—we call it the hall but it's more of a balcony or catwalk—I would look down into the first-floor living area and see the antique couch we just reupholstered, the coffee table littered with catalogs and unread magazines, and the kitchen table where Nicholas spreads office papers in a little nest of statistics and sales figures. He's busy working long hours these days, paying for this house, and the architects, and the couch and oriental rugs, and the greenhouse where I grow flowering ivy and cherry tomatoes that are sweet enough to pop in your mouth like candy.

With both hands gripping the rail, head craned forward, I'm reminded of zoo exhibits where people gaze down at the re-created habitats of bears and tigers. From this vantage point I can see all the messes we've left behind: the neglected dinner dishes spattered with marinara, the shoes and balled-up socks Nicholas shed while reading the paper, my unfinished solitaire game. If I were to turn away from these things, I would stand face-to-face with his painting hanging on the wall behind me. Funny how I see it as his painting now.

Let me show you the aerial view, he says when he brings visitors up to the second floor, but it's really the painting he wants to show. *It's the only thing I've ever painted,* he says, *but it's pretty good, don't you think?* Then they look harder, trying to discern the hidden messages in the blacks and grays. Objects that might be faces float and swirl and blend, and the only brightness is a sliver of yellow in one corner, like a door opening or closing.

They look and they look some more, and then he tells them the story. At least he tells them part of the story. He says, *It was a difficult period in our life,* the way he might say *our car, our sofa, our house.* But it is his painting. It is his story. He says to me, *You remember, don't you?*

Yes, I remember. I smile and say, *Oh, sure,* but I want to tell him, *Yes, yes, and he's probably passed away by now, you know. He had cancer.* Nicholas does not know this, at least not in words, although I'm guessing that somewhere at the back of his brain he knows something like it. How could he look at that painting and not know? Although maybe the painting is simply like an embarrassing photograph of himself taken at a particular time and place. Maybe his story is that seamless.

"No," he might say. "I didn't know that."

When I told my brother what Nicholas had done, he changed seats at the kitchen table so that he could be closer to me. He left his coffee behind at his first seat, and I looked at it instead of him as I talked, as if he were still seated there. The mug was decorated with a primitive cartoon of a cowboy and cowgirl square dancing, and I remember wondering how such a stupid thing had infiltrated my life.

"Larry," I said, "don't get upset. It's nothing. He went to work today, and I talked to him at lunch. Everything's fine."

"Are you okay?" he asked.

"Yes, I think so," I said.

This was more than a year ago, when Nicholas was still trying to scratch and claw his way out of the Nashua branch of his company. We were in the old house then, near Larry's mail route, and he sometimes dropped by in the afternoons, still in uniform with mail still in his bag, wanting to rest his feet and chat with his sister. So that day was nothing unusual except for the story I had to tell.

"Are you sure?" Larry asked with a tone of demand, and I remembered how he had once been in a fight over money out in Oregon and punched a man so hard he had broken two of his own fingers along with the other man's jaw. This all happened when he had been drinking, and there was shame and repentance in his voice when he told me later. Now he had

three years of AA under his belt, and he was passing me a handkerchief with the hand that had been broken.

"Yes," I said. "I'm sure."

He smiled tightly and said, "Are you *sure* sure or just sure?"
trying to tease a laugh out of me, I guess, or to dig deeper.
"You're not sure," he said when I didn't answer.

They were friendly but certainly not friends, my brother and
my husband. Nicholas had once referred to Larry as "my luna-
tic brother-in-law" after they had an argument about politics.
He had said it with a smile but with an edge too, and now Larry
spoke with the same edge when he said, "You have to protect
yourself in a situation like this."

"Protect myself from what?"

"Well, he's violent," Larry said, and for a second I wanted to
take back what I had told him and hide it in some small corner
of my mind, away from even myself.

We talked more, but I wanted to be alone, and pretty soon
Larry was saying good-bye and he would call me in the morning. Nicholas would be coming soon, or at least that's what
Larry thought, and it dawned on me as I was hugging him that
this was part of why he was leaving. What would have happened if they had been standing in the same room right then?

I watched from the window as Larry climbed into his mail
truck and headed off to complete his route. I wondered how
many letters he must deliver a day. Not form letter come-ons,
not junk mail or bills or magazines, but personal correspon-
dence written in somebody's own handwriting, from one mind
to another. Right then that kind of communication seemed
quaint, the way most things do when they're tipping toward
extinction, and I suddenly wished Nicholas had written me
long, impassioned letters in his own hand when we had been
courting, when I was twenty-one and he was twenty-nine and

a new life seemed like something you could slide into like our new swimming pool. I suppose I wanted a reminder of that time now that all the roses were dead, the expensive dinners eaten and digested and gone to my hips. Or maybe I just wanted to write a letter myself.

"Describe it," I told Nicholas when he called me from his hotel room across town. I had been trying to sleep and pretend that the incident with the hammer was just a dream my subconscious had burped up. But the ring of the phone and a glance at the clock reminded me that it had been not only something that actually happened—it had happened that very day.

"What?" he asked.

"Describe it," I repeated.

The possibility occurred to me that Nicholas had set out running somewhere further—New York City, some shadowy ex-girlfriend's place—and ended up at the hotel owing to lack of ambition as much as anything else. The whole thing seemed silly. Beneath us.

"How does it feel?" I asked. "Tell me."

"It's just stress," he said.

There was no puzzle to a word like that. You could solve it by change of habit or act of will, by *simply getting your ass in gear,* which is what Larry did when he sobered up, moved out here, and began his second stint as a government employee. I said, "I want to know."

"It feels *stressful,*" Nicholas said, and he laughed the clipped laugh he had laughed the night before when he first saw me watching him, just before he raised the hammer.

"Please," I said. A girlishness had entered my voice. A pleading quality. I remembered the weightlessness of my body in our early days, when first twisting under the sheets in his bed; I felt a similar buoyancy now, except I was alone. The light was out in the bedroom, and I was spread across the top of the blanket in my clothes, and I knew this was how I would fall asleep that night and wake the next day. I said, "You need to tell me. I'm your wife."

He sighed and there was silence on the other end of the line, except the television in the background—a movie or something competing with our own little drama. He said, "I don't know."

"It feels like you're keeping a secret from me," I said. "It's like you're having an affair." I brought my legs to my stomach and listened to the muffled sounds of his television playing on the other side of town. "It's like you're having an affair with your sadness."

"It's not sadness," he said. "And don't be so over-the-top. If you want to help somebody, help yourself."

I chose to ignore that. "Well, then *you* tell *me* what it is," I said, and I wished so much that he was not there in that blank, clean room watching a movie from his bed. I wanted to touch him and look into his eyes and read the secrets there. If not for the television I would have been listening to nothing at all.

Finally he said, "It's like voices talking in my head. Not talking really. More like mumbling. So I can only hear certain things they're telling me . . . Now *I'm* the one getting melodramatic. Is this what you wanted? Did you want to hear that your husband has little voices in his head?" He was angry now, like the night before in the cellar, and I gripped the phone and listened. "Here's another way to put it. My thoughts get ahead of me."

The television was quieter. Music was playing. A commercial or something. I could hear him breathing, and it seemed a message was in that faint sound if only I could listen hard enough.

"It's like my thoughts separate from me," he said.

I should have been the one to leave, I realized. "And that's what happened last night?" I asked. "Your thoughts separated from you?"

I remembered something I had seen as a child: bats scattering from the shadow of a tree and moving in a million different directions. A second before, the tree had looked solid and whole. Then the bats burst into motion. It was as if the tree had exploded itself by magic and sent its branches into the sky over my head.

"I guess," he said.

What should I have said? That he needed to open himself up to a psychiatrist? Should I have told him to stay away from me or to please come home? I said what I felt. I said, "We should go away, Nicholas." I said, "Let's just get out of here. I want to go far away."

We had tried, I had tried, to put my finger on the problem for a while now, but it was getting worse, not better. I wanted to escape. I wanted back the man I knew, that difficult, sardonic, and capable man, the man who talked and talked about his day and the incompetents he had to put up with, who ate greedily by scraping his fork across his plate and kissed me that way too, as if he thought he might have to break into a run. That man seemed farther away than across town in a Best Western.

"We need to go away," I said, and suddenly the problem seemed almost that simple.

"I know," he said. "I've been looking at some pamphlets. There's a place in upstate New York. They drop you off in a cabin in the woods, and you chop your own firewood and become one with nature." His voice was flat. I didn't know if he was serious or joking.

"A vacation," I said, which was not what I had meant. It

seemed like his gift to me, the way the comforter I was lying on had been a gift, and the stupid little literacy meetings, and the admission that his thoughts could be so out of control. I said, "That doesn't sound like a good idea."

"It's not a vacation. Not really. It's a program. That's a word the pamphlets use a lot. *Program* and *system*."

It occurred to me that he was looking at these pamphlets as we talked and hoping that at least one of the yoga centers, mountain hideaways, or relaxation tours contained an answer. It didn't occur to me then that a drowning person, flailing around for anything to hold onto, might hurt those who were trying hardest to help. I could hear a trace of stand-up comedian shtick in his voice when he said, "Calling it a program or a system makes it sound more important. Weight-loss programs, for instance. Whole health system. Motivation systems. Ketchup release systems."

I couldn't help but laugh. "Fine," I said. "Fine. Let's go. We'll play horseshoes and meditate and do aromatherapy."

"I don't want to do any of that," he said, and his voice was flat again as if a switch had been flipped. "I want to go on walks though. With you. And I'd like to paint. They do some interesting stuff with painting." And he began to read to me from one of the pamphlets, describing a place in Vermont called Harborage Creative Retreats, where there were staff counselors and art teachers and more than thirty acres of forest conveniently located near a major interstate.

Before I quit my job, my students and I would meet on Sunday mornings in the damp basement of the public library and fumble through dog-eared books. They sipped their coffees and smoked cigarettes standing at the window, and they listened and then I listened, and we made our way through a slew of children's books and three novels this way. I have not read a single novel in the six months since I left the adult literacy program, and those three books are still vivid in my mind: the horror story, the hyperbolic romance, and the transcontinental spy drama.

But what I remember most is the stories the students told. It seemed incredible that people who struggled through a newspaper could tell such amazing stories: living in rural Canada during World War II, mothering ten children, hitchhiking across America. If they were jealous of my nice clothes and my courage in the face of the English language, then I was equally jealous of their stories and the courage they displayed in them. "I need a break," I eventually told Nicholas. "I'm not very good at it. And Sunday should be our day, don't you think?"

He made a half-spoken sound like he was eating something sticky. It was his salary that had put me in the position of being able to volunteer, and I think he considered it his work almost as much as mine. Perhaps he got more out of it than I did. He was hunched over his papers, and he reminded me of my students when they squinted and puzzled over their books as if what they saw there was disgusting in its complexity.

This was a couple of weeks after we returned from Vermont with the painting, and a couple of months before he received his promotion and we began to talk to the architects in New Haven. Nicholas said he was doing great now. The dark days had passed over our heads like birds. We both must have felt it even then, the pulling inward of our lives into something smaller and harder.

As usual the story Harborage Creative Retreats had told about itself was different than the reality. We were first greeted by a sign at the end of a dirt driveway, then by a woman who said her name was Bobbie. She was director of the place, she explained, and had been for almost ten years. Her hair was frizzy with humidity, her flower-print dress shapelessly baggy. She had the look of someone stumbling to the end of the day as if to a finish line.

The old Victorian house behind her, the place where she said the art studios were located, was painted white and had a vaguely institutional feel. A black fire escape climbed one side like a vine. Bobbie was smiling tight-lipped, like she had something to hide.

"You look *stressed*," Nicholas told her, and then he looked at me and grinned, although the smile was like hers, forced and almost grotesque. She led us through the house, past someone in running shorts talking on a cell phone and a woman yelling at her kids. "I didn't know there were going to be children here," Nicholas said. "What do they need art therapy for? They can play video games to get out their aggression."

He smiled and tilted his head up and off to the side as if to avoid a smell, and I thought of a line he sometimes used when we talked about plans for a family. *I'm my own child*, he would say. I wondered if he was my child too. Maybe I was his. The kids ran past us out onto the back lawn, probably to find things to climb on, throw, and break.

The back rooms smelled of damp and Lysol and something fishy from the kitchen, where a couple of people were sitting around drinking coffee and eating what looked like birthday cake. We passed them and walked into another room, where picnic tables were lined in rows and primitive paintings covered the walls. It reminded me of a kindergarten classroom.

Nicholas had vanished, headed off to the bathroom or on solo recon duty.

"Who is that?" I asked.

On the other side of the room a man sat alone at a table, working a large mound of clay. He was so pale and tall and slender as to appear mismatched to his stool and table, the room, and my assumptions about this place. The people in the hall had a robust glow that seemed a sign of what Harborage Creative Retreats could do for a person who gave the process a chance. But this man definitely looked ill. He looked like he needed help.

"Oh," Bobbie said, "that's Unger," as if this would explain everything. Then she called out to him. "Unger," she said, "there's someone here I want you to meet."

He glanced at us with his large watery eyes and smiled slightly, seemingly with effort and pain. It looked a little like he was flinching.

"This is Carol," Bobbie hollered. She was talking slowly, as if Unger were deaf or foreign or simply dim-witted. He held up his palm in a wave, and I saw how big his hand was, although I still wasn't sure how big the whole man was. He was hunching, kind of folded up on his stool. He closed his hand and returned to his work.

"He's dying," Bobbie explained to me as we walked out by the man-made pond.

I awoke late that night in a room that smelled of lemon air freshener to find myself alone. I remember not knowing what to do with the empty space next to me, if I should ignore it, if I should decide it was a gift and kick my legs across it and fall back asleep. Nicholas had been doing this kind of thing lately, heading off at night to fast-food restaurants or malls. I decided he was probably driving around aimlessly or maybe walking in the moonlight. With the image of Nicholas trudging along a woodland trail occupying my mind, I decided to get dressed and make the best of my wakefulness.

I found a blank canvas in the commons area, set it on an easel, and began to paint without plan or intention. I had a brush dabbed with blue, and I moved it back and forth in one corner until I had created an awkward sense of sky. Then I painted the opposite corner green for grass and began on the middle. I don't know what magic I expected to flow from me into the brush and out onto the canvas, but I was ready to give up when someone came up behind me. "That's wonderful," he said. It was Unger.

"Jesus, you scared me," I told him, although I was laughing a little. I looked back at the painting, hoping to see it with new eyes. I had crosshatched a grainy square at the center of the canvas. It looked vaguely threatening somehow, mainly because it did not belong between the blue and green. Maybe that's the quality Unger had noticed.

"It's awful," I said, and I scrunched up my nose at it. It was a genuine reaction. I wasn't trying to illicit anything.

"No, really," he said, "it's nice."

"You're backtracking," I said. "In a second you'll be telling me that it's interesting." But he looked puzzled by this, so I said, "Thanks. That's very sweet of you to say."

"You're here alone," he said.

I didn't know if he meant here in this room, or here at the house. "That's right," I said.

"Me too," he said, and he looked at my brush. All the other

brushes were clean. Leaving my brush stained in paint suddenly seemed like a heartless thing to do, and I picked up the brush and walked over to the tap. It was a deep sink with colored stains spattered at the bottom, and I felt more artistic standing there than in front of the easel. "Can I show you how to wash the brush?" he asked, when he saw what I was doing.

I handed it to him, and he held it under the tap and passed his fingers across it gently, always in the same direction. I realized then that I had taken the place I had seen him sitting earlier that day, and that it was probably his brush and his canvas that I had been using. In fact, I thought, this was probably his time to be here alone. I had taken that from him as well.

I looked around the room at the confusion of half-finished paintings and asked him which ones were his, although I knew without being told. The good ones, the ones with a point of view. The one on the far wall. The painting of a thin gray body curled in on itself against a background of small circles. The one of identical houses separated by a small river. "A good number of these are mine," he said.

"You must paint a lot," I said.

"Yes," he said. "It's good for me." He smiled slightly, as if remembering something soft and sentimental. "I don't usually have these kinds of resources. I run an audiovisual department at a boarding school not far from here. It's a good job, but it's not a very good outlet for my creativity."

"Sure," I said.

"What do you do?" he asked.

"I teach," I said. I knew the picture I was putting in his mind. I couldn't help myself.

"You must really enjoy that," he said, and then he narrowed

his eyes and looked over what I had done. He said, "If you don't mind I'd like to add to what you've done." He leaned in close to the easel like he was looking for something and then ran the brush across it. He added to what I had done—transformed it—and for a second I almost told him to stop, because I thought he might cover up my work completely. He said, "I'm adding texture."

"You're ill," I said.

"Yes," he said, as he smudged the brush around in the color, "although I wasn't ill when I first started coming here. Can you believe that? I was just a little down. I became sick later. Strange, don't you think? Bobbie and I joke about that."

All of this he said in a slow, methodical way, as if sharing even this skeletal information was somehow painful. I wanted to ask him that as well. Was he in pain? Physical pain, I mean. There was a bruise on his neck about the size and shape of a fried egg, yellow at the center, bleeding into red and purple that darkened to near black at the outer edge. I told myself not to pay attention to it, but then I said, "That looks like it hurts."

"Oh, that," he said, and he touched it. "It's just ugly, that's all."

"It's kind of interesting," I said. For some reason it reminded me of the paintings. The dense discoloration of it. A certain combination of accident and intention. I looked at it more closely. "Can I touch it?" I asked. Touching it meant touching him.

"It's just a bruise," he said, but when I reached out he craned his neck slightly, and I rested two fingers against it. I could feel his blood pumping.

I took my hand away and let it fall to my side. "I'm sorry," I said. "I'm kind of at the end of my tether right now."

He made a small hmm, signifying understanding maybe, and moved the brush in a zigzag. He smiled bashfully again. "I think I might be at the end of my tether too. Maybe I should just go to bed."

"Maybe I should too," I said. I stood up to leave, but that was all. He turned to the canvas, and I watched him dab the brush and make a long stroke of aquamarine along the center. I told myself, *he is not a painter, not really,* and as I told myself this, I heard a noise behind me. Not a noise so much as a feeling. I turned but nobody was there, so I walked out into the hall. I might have seen someone walking back to the cabins—a figure moving into the woods at a steady pace—although, of course, I could have been seeing things.

I thought about Nicholas and the hammer. The simple act of remembering that night seemed an offense again him, but how could I help it? I went onto the porch and looked harder for the shape of something human. One of those double swing things was hanging there suspended by sturdy chains. I hadn't noticed it before. It looked like the kind of seat in which you could pass a whole evening, and I almost put both hands to my mouth and shouted for my husband so we could sit there together.

As I swung back and forth I thought about a man in my reading group who had lost a thumb and finger to a badger when he was thirteen. I had admired him and joked with him about his French Canadian accent, and I had felt my heart fill with embarrassment and pity when he first stumbled through a Dick and Jane book. I thought of Unger and his paintbrush and how I had touched his neck and then run away like a child playing tag.

It was a beautiful night, and with the wide expanse of lawn and dogwood trees lit by floodlights the whole world looked like it had been set down by an artist's hand.

"I'm always getting screwed for other people's incompetence," Nicholas said, which was as close as I'd heard him come to swearing.

He had come through the door holding his tie in his hand and smelling of sweat and cigarettes. One of his two big accounts was falling through. The navy account or the 3M account, I don't remember. Nicholas didn't tell me much about what had happened, because he said he had things to do down in the cellar. There was this bookcase he was making. Carpentry was something he had been trying out the last couple of months, along with swimming laps.

I was loading the dishwasher, listening to the banging of the hammer and hoping that the phone would ring and rescue me from the dirty pans. He had left his tie and jacket over the back of a chair, but he still wore the rest of his office clothes, which seemed sloppy and almost arrogant—a disruption of the patterns we had created together for five years and grown to expect.

There was a stop-start rhythm to the sound of his work. The hammer would bang two or three times, grow quiet, start up again, then stop. I imagined the nail bending sideways, Nicholas tapping it back into position, then bending it again or knocking it crooked. He was probably getting annoyed.

Some men can drive a nail in two or three solid blows. My brother is one of them, and Nicholas knows this. He's seen him do it. I'm not bad with my hands either, although I don't use them often except when gardening. I wanted to take the hammer from him and drive the nail myself, but instead I took the plates we had eaten our dinner on the night before and set them out for our dinner again. They were blue with a silver ring around the edge. Clean and with a carefully prepared meal on them, they looked like something you would photograph for an expensive magazine.

The hammer was silent now. I listened for Nicholas's feet clomping on the stairs, but that's not the sound I heard. Instead I heard a heavy metallic clang, once, then again, and again. It was a trash can. He had knocked the trash can over. I'm not sure why, but I finished loading the dishwasher, three or four glasses and a coffee mug, which I placed upside down on the top rack. Then I grabbed a towel and walked to the top of the cellar stairs, where I dried my hands. The plates were on the sideboard. I had a duck in the oven and a honey sauce simmering on the stove, and I wanted to cry because I should have expected this.

The hammer started up again, faster now, six or seven times. It quickened as it clattered away. There is a certain sound that metal against metal makes, and this wasn't that sound. I walked down the stairs to the first landing and bent to look. I could smell sawdust and turpentine, and I realized that this was the first time in months I had come into the cellar.

The wood had already split, but he kept hitting it. He was smashing the top of the bookcase. And although his arm was pumping hard, he wore the most casual expression, as if he were still driving a nail. His white Oxford was open, and I could see his bare chest and belly. "Jesus, Nicholas," I said.

"I banged my fucking hand." He held the hammer out to me, head first, I'm not sure why. Then he tossed it across the room at the washing machine. It hit dead center with a loud bang, so that the machine shook. He was better at throwing the hammer than at driving nails with it.

His mouth was bent at one side in a half grin, and when he looked at me I thought, you don't recognize me, do you? Of course he did recognize me. He must have. But that's what I thought. The look in his eyes reminded me of a dog I saw once hit by a car and limping in a circle.

Nicholas would call that kind of comparison melodramatic. He might view it as a lie. I think if I had said something then he might have stopped, but I didn't, and he walked across the room and picked up the hammer and drove the claw through the unfinished wallboard behind the washer. He yanked and pulled back a couple of times jerking the hammer free and then sent it in again, deeper this time, like he was digging for something. I was just a witness now. I was watching long-distance. He drove six or seven holes through the wall and then turned and threw the hammer again. It skidded across the concrete floor and hit the stairs.

I flinched. I had thought for a second—I had *known*—that he was throwing it at me. I had been absolutely sure. My worry for him became worry for myself, and for the duck in the oven and the relaxing evening I had planned. If he had wanted me to scream or run or grab his wrist and tell him to stop, I realized then that it was something I couldn't give.

He kicked over the bookcase, but that was it. He was done. There was that calm, satisfied look on his face, in his eyes. As if he was pleased with what he had accomplished. And it did feel that way even to me. Behind the fear there was that feeling of *yes, we've finished what we started, we've finished the performance*. Something about it seemed orchestrated. I thought about the duck again, which I would rescue in plenty of time and eat with my husband of five years while we watched a black-and-white movie.

He bent over and righted the bookcase, but something about that must have seemed incorrect, so he gave it a nudge and let it fall again. My brother would later call it a temper tantrum. Which was so right and so wrong at the same time. Because of course there was more to it. Maybe Nicholas simply wanted me to see. That's the measure of any performance—how much you touch the audience.

I stood up and looked at him and he looked at me, and I wondered if he could do something like break my arm the way Larry had broken that man's jaw in Oregon. I said, "I want you to spend the night somewhere else tonight."

"I had already decided that. I'm going to a hotel," he said, and with one sentence he made my demand his decision. I almost asked him to stay then, but I just walked back upstairs.

How long had Larry lived with the shame of breaking that man's jaw? I wanted to tell my friends, neighbors, and family that my husband was capable of causing just that kind of hurt—the kind that people understand. I had evidence, didn't I? I know marriages that have ended over less. I could hear him sweeping splinters of wood and dust across the floor, but I didn't go to help. I remember thinking, he's the one who made the mess, he can clean it up. I picked up one of the plates and debated throwing it, but the act seemed so meager and ill timed that instead I scooped string beans onto it, then a strip of duck, and brought it to the table.

"Where have you been, stranger?" I asked Nicholas late the next morning when I found him in our room staring into the bathroom mirror and running a razor across his cheek.

I had just returned from a lecture on the muse and the id and the importance of the lived life. Bobbie had told me that *they*—meaning men, meaning husbands, meaning the depressed and sick-of-heart, meaning I-have-no-idea-what—often took two steps back after their first step forward. "Love is a powerful tool during this time," she had explained, and I had wished I was back in my house where my love seemed stronger, propped up by the familiar, and not here where I had to listen to her tell me about ceramics while my husband was apparently still out roaming in the woods like a werewolf.

But seeing him shaving at the mirror made me think he had simply spent the night in another Best Western. "Here and there," he said out of the side of his mouth. "Here and there," and he rinsed the razor and tapped it on the sink. "What have I learned so far?" he asked himself aloud. "That mental health is a state of mind." He wiped off his face and plopped on the bed and dug his hand into a bag of someone else's chocolate chip cookies that he must have taken from the kitchen. He smelled of cigarette smoke and shaving cream and pine trees, and I knew he was ready to take off and hike around the house for another hour if I said the wrong thing.

"You're not doing too well, are you?" I asked.

"Not really," he said, although he was still smiling. I stood in front of the sink and scrubbed liquid soap into my face and smoothed it around. "I don't know who I am anymore," he said after a while, quiet enough that for a second it seemed as if he could have said something else entirely. I thought, *You're Nicholas, damn it, my husband. Remember?* He said, "Maybe I don't know who *you* are. Maybe that's what it is." I filled my hands with water and splashed my face and then fumbled around for a towel. It was not as if I was ignoring him. I was just ill pre-pared. He said, "I need help, you know."

"That's why we're here," I said, and hearing my own words almost made me laugh.

"No," he said. "I need *your* help." He was behind me now. I could see his face in the mirror. He had been crying, I think. He smiled when I took the towel away from my face, and waved with his fingers. "I see you," he said in a baby voice.

I said, "I don't understand this. We're doing okay. You're doing okay, and I'm doing okay. We're supposed to be content. This shouldn't be happening."

His hand wandered to his face and found an ugly little razor cut. It ran from the top of his lip to his nostril, and it was begin-ning to bleed. He rubbed the blood away with his finger. "Let's run away," he said. "Let's run away now."

"We did run away," I said. "That's why we're here."

But he looked at me hard, and the matter was settled. I jerked open the closet and took out my suitcase, the new one I had bought two weeks earlier for some better vacation, and threw it on the bed. He stood and watched as if this were all my deci-sion, and I wanted to go to him and run my fingers through his hair. Instead I popped open the latches. The suitcase opened its mouth to me. Would we keep doing this forever, running from place to place to place as if pursued by something invis-ible and stealthy and single-minded? I said, "You better save me one of those cookies."

He said, "You're keeping something from me."

"You're keeping something from me," I said.

"Then I guess we're even," he said, and he handed me a cookie as we walked to the car. People were watching from the windows, I was sure. "Just throw it on the backseat," he said and opened the door for me to toss in the suitcase. I glanced back at the house and wondered which room was Unger's and if he was asleep or awake and what made Nicholas want to leave so quickly and quietly as if we were thieves. Which is, of course, what we were.

The morning after we returned from Vermont I was awakened by someone knocking on the back door. It was Larry. He had driven by to check on the house and seen our car parked in the driveway. "Is everything okay?" he asked, when I came to the door, and he looked over my shoulder for Nicholas, who was still sleeping upstairs.

"Oh, sure," I said. We had coffee, and I put out some plates, although we didn't have time to put food on them, because Nicholas came downstairs and wanted to unload the car. He had been too tired the night before.

"I have something to show you," he told Larry, and he walked around the car and opened the trunk, and there it was. He hefted it upright for us to see. A painting. Brown landscape with what might have been a tree in one corner, a tree or a man, staring at the ground and thinking about something. It was Unger's. The one he had painted that night in the studio, the one I began and he finished.

Larry looked it over from side to side, and I knew what he was doing: simultaneously looking Nicholas over as well, trying to fit this new piece into the puzzle that was his sister's husband.

"It's very good," he finally said, and I agreed. It seemed like exactly the kind of painting that Nicholas would have rendered if he'd had the inclination or ability. The abstract little tree-man, the wide swaths of unadorned ground, and what looked like a fire now, beneath the ground, or a red river. It was hard to tell, because the perspective was off.

That's right, I thought, that's the reason we went, wasn't it? To make something we could bring back and show around like a photograph, displaying us in new contexts. I pushed something down inside myself, the way you sometimes push trash down in the can until it is hard and dense at the bottom of the bag. I said, "You can bring it through the front. It's easier that way. Be careful."

Larry took the painting from Nicholas. He had to hold his arms apart, it was that wide. "What's it called?" he asked.

"I don't know," Nicholas said. "Call it whatever you want. A rose by any other name, right?"

Larry shifted it in his hands to get a better grip and held it up to the sun. "This is really very good," he said, and I knew what he was thinking: that he had been wrong or at least not completely right.

I was thinking the same thing. Because as Unger's painting it was simply not that great, but seeing it through Larry's eyes as Nicholas's painting, it was surprisingly good. It wasn't the artistic breakthrough Unger had been looking for, but it was Nicholas's breakthrough now, and as he told my brother the story of our weekend, I thought of my own awkward stabs at the canvas, so small and unnecessary next to my husband's success.

Which is why tonight when I am restless I move my hand down his chest to the inside of his thigh where the skin is pale and hairless. I shake him gently, trying to push through his dream, and he makes a sound at the back of his throat. An animal grunt. He doesn't know who I am—he recognizes me as a noise, a push, a discomfort, something outside the darkness of his rest. I climb out of bed, and I go to the hall. I am going to clean up the mess downstairs. That's my intention at first, but then I decide to clean the top floor. That's how it starts. That's how the painting ends up off the wall, raised above my head.

He'll hear the noise as if from some distant place, the way I first heard the hammer. He's not sleeping that soundly.